FLOWERS
in
DECEMBER

Rick Tenmoo

authorHOUSE

AuthorHouse™
1663 Liberty Drive
Bloomington, IN 47403
www.authorhouse.com
Phone: 833-262-8899

Published by AuthorHouse 08/07/2023

ISBN: 979-8-8230-1304-8 (sc)
ISBN: 979-8-8230-1303-1 (e)

Library of Congress Control Number: 2023914867

Print information available on the last page.

Any people depicted in stock imagery provided by Getty Images are models, and such images are being used for illustrative purposes only. Certain stock imagery © Getty Images.

This book is printed on acid-free paper.

To my wife, Lisa, the love of my life, my biggest fan, and my truly motivational muse for the writing of this story. She inspired me to rise to a higher level of understanding of myself and the world in which we all live and to grow that inner strength that we all have but sometimes never find the courage and energy to develop.

A special dedication to my mother, Ludell, who has always been an incredible source of courage and taught me what I needed to know to be a decent, respectful human being, and to my two sisters, Patrease and Faith, who were always there when I needed them most to provide the support and encouragement that only sisters can provide.

Just when we think we have
figured out this thing called
life, we are immediately tested
to see what we really know.

The snow came early this year in Michigan. During the past few years, we had been lucky and had only some scattered, light dusting starting in late November, but this year the big storms were arriving early to remind me that I lived just a thirty-minute car ride from Canada and that it was cold as shit in this part of the country. I had only been back a few days from my mad-dash trip to Virginia, and I was still exhausted, physically and emotionally. Loss has always been hard for me, and the thought of having to go back only depressed me that much more. While I was never a true Michigander and never fully appreciated the bone-chilling weather, I did finally resign myself to the reality that I would be in this state for a while anyway, having made the place my home for more than fifteen years. The fatigue made me take two weeks off from work as soon as I returned, as I considered myself woefully unfit to be around anybody in a work environment. And yet for another moment in my life, I felt the sting of losing someone close to me. I felt out of focus with the world, out of sync with the ebbs and flows of my normal life experiences. I believed that I would never be completely right for a long time, if ever.

Like many people dealing with loss, I tried to understand and make sense of why people died as I attempted to rationalize a completely irrational occurrence. These thoughts only led to an overwhelming feeling of injustice and anger. Anger because something about the randomness of dying from anything other than old age seemed so completely unfair, even though I knew there was nothing fair about life or death. And for most of my life, I'd never expected or really believed that life, in all its different iterations and forms, had anything to do with what was fair, what was right, or what was just. But when confronting it on a deeply personal level, I couldn't help but feel the unfairness of life, the randomness of it all. I knew deep down that it was the grief driving these depressing, metaphysical thoughts, but I still had them all the same.

Why did some people die young, and why did decent, good people die in some of the most horrible ways imaginable, while those damn hell-raisers seemed to live forever, wreaking havoc on everybody and everything around them? Ultimately, I knew there were no satisfying answers. In life everybody and everything was fair game, and while we tended to live like we knew what was going to happen even in the next moment, the truth was that we didn't. And so I was like everyone else, completely caught off guard when the unimaginable happened suddenly and reminded me that I really lived in an anything-can-happen world, that my days were numbered, and that I had no idea when or even how I was going to die—unless I got a terminal disease, and that was even more depressing. There were so many things I didn't get to say, conversations that now would never happen, and experiences that would never occur. No nostalgic walks down memory lane, no remember-when stories shared at a class reunion about the things we did in our youth and all the things we had done since. Death moved people beyond our reach forever, and we were left to figure things out as best we could and hang on to whatever loving memories we had collected over the years because there would be no new ones from the people we lost.

And I so desperately tried to drag my thoughts into the present and to live in the individual moments that I was living in right now, but my feelings kept dragging me back to the past, to the last few days and the hospital visit, the crying, the pain, the anger, and the disappointment—thoughts that were too fresh to be filed away but too painful to feel. I was hurting and had absolutely no clue how to get past the painful mental pictures that kept playing over and over in my mind, and like so many others, I wallowed in it, living through days in pajamas and eating peanut butter out of a jar for breakfast and dinner, not shaving or maintaining any other personal hygiene care whatsoever, staying up half the night and then sleeping through the day and wondering when I would find the strength and the courage to go back to Virginia for a funeral I didn't want to attend, for more emotional suffering I didn't know if I had the capacity to deal with.

On the third day back, I found myself lying in bed, staring at the ceiling, and wanting so desperately to fall asleep, to ease my suffering through slumber, but sleep would not come yet on this night. I decided that I had to do something other than lie in bed being sad and pathetic. I got up on this sad-sack Tuesday around one o'clock in the morning. I felt the frustration rising in me, as sleep was apparently not visiting me anytime soon; those damn sleeping sheep were nowhere to be found, and the lack of sleep only added to my misery. I had been lying in bed for the last three hours watching my mental pictures: smiling faces filled with laughter at a college bowling party, stories being shared in a dorm room about a bad date, hospital beds and nurses dressed in white, crying faces, and tubes and bedside machines that made that eerie sound of human breathing. The pictures played over and over again in my head, and if I could control my mental mind guy, I would

4

have choked his ass to death for causing me so much pain and suffering. I felt so incredibly stuck, so hopelessly lost. I climbed out of bed and walked over to the window. My blinds were closed, but light seeped in around the edges and through the spaces between the individual blinds. It wasn't a lot of light, but it was enough to be annoying on sleepless nights. I opened the blinds and looked out the window at the quietness of the night.

Everything looked frozen in time, and the effect was only heightened by the white covering of snow that created that crystal snow globe effect during Michigan winters. A parking lot lamp cast light on the cars closest to the building, and I could see my black GM Sonic parked next to the handicapped space closest to the walkway. I loved that space for the very reason that I could see my car from my second-floor window. In my mind, I always felt that if someone tried to steal it, I would hear them, spring out of bed, and scare them off by yelling obscenities through the window. The truth was if someone stole my car, they would be truly hard-pressed as the lot was filled with newer, more expensive vehicles than mine. As a matter of fact, a Dodge Charger was parked in the handicapped space, and the custom tires on that car were probably worth more than my whole car. And what kind of disabled person drove a Charger anyway? Another young person too lazy to walk a few feet from the parking lot, using a space they shouldn't be in.

These were my wandering, meaningless thoughts on an early Tuesday morning as I stared out my bedroom window to pass the time on another sleepless night. Then I saw a couple coming from a section of the lot farther from the building. They were young and walked hand in hand, wrapped in the warmth of long winter coats and appropriately matching boots, gloves, and hats. They were talking loudly and laughing. Alcohol might have been involved, but they seemed happy, and wherever they had come from must have been one hell of a party. They moved with an ease and casualness only reserved for the young. I watched with some sense of envy of their youth, their vitality, and their seemingly carefree movements. I remembered when I was one of those young, amazing, throw-caution-to-the-wind kind of people. But my time had passed, and my youth was well in my rearview mirror, and I was a middle-aged man living in a two-bedroom apartment with nothing more meaningful to do than to stare out the window and ruminate about the vicissitudes of living and the misery of eventually dying.

I watched the couple until they disappeared up a long walkway, heading to the eastern part of the apartment complex. Their talk and laughter faded until the peaceful silence was restored and nothing moved under the covering of the white winter coating on a dark winter's night.

I stared out for another twenty minutes or so, and then I went into the living room area and turned on the TV. This night, like others of recent, would end with me finally falling asleep in my football recliner while the unwatched TV flashed pictures of those ubiquitous late-night infomercials interspersed with one of those made-for-TV movies.

When we are at our lowest in life, that's the time for the greatest opportunity for personal growth and enlightenment.

My eyes opened slowly, and I squinted at the piercing sunlight from my kitchen window. My living and dining rooms were one big continuous space. During the night I had left the blinds down, but they were still open. It didn't matter at night because it was dark, and no outside light was visible on that side of my apartment building, but when the sun rose and the blinds were left open, the streaming sunlight overwhelmed my cheap plastic blinds and always forced me to look down to the floor until my eyes adjusted after I'd fallen asleep watching television. The remote sat on the floor next to my chair where I must have dropped it during the night, and I heard the sound of someone running and screaming coming from a TV that had watched me more than I had watched it. I slowly picked up the remote and promptly turned the TV off. Silence.

I tried to focus my mind on the next thing I needed to do but then decided that I didn't have a next thing and so I sat in silence and tried not to think. This silent moment was working until it was abruptly interrupted after a few minutes by my ringing cell phone. My ringer was loud and annoying, and I made a mental note to turn it to vibrate after this particular call. I could hear it but couldn't remember where it was. Looking around, it had to be close. Duh! It was on the floor on the other side of the chair.

Andrea's name flashed on the screen.

"Hello," I said with all the energy of a sobering drunk.

"Thomas, how you doing?" she asked.

I could sense the sincerity in her voice. I should have said something to actually answer the question, but the sleepy, unfocused me said, "Why you calling so early? I'm just waking up."

"Cause it's 2:30 p.m. and early was over about three hours ago," she responded.

"Oh!" was all I could say.

"How you doing, Thomas?" she asked again, in that same caring tone she had used earlier.

Andrea Fullwood was my ex-wife of five years. After we divorced, we understandably lost touch, but the breakup wasn't one of those acrimonious burn-the-house-to-the-ground types of events. She came to me one day while I was watching a football game in our living room and simply said, "This ain't working for me, Thomas." And that was the beginning of the end for us, and I could hardly disagree. Somewhere after that third year, I felt like I was living with a stranger. Outwardly, we appeared to be another successful couple pursuing our dreams in life. Yet inwardly we had parted ways and become very different people wanting different things out of life. Our relationship had become one of routine, both of us moving and doing but not really connecting or caring. After some time had passed, we became friends and realized that we were much better at that type of relationship than when we were married.

"OK," I found myself saying, wanting to end this line of conversation before it went down the road of emotional feelings and phrases like "It's OK to cry" and "I miss her too" talk. I went silent, refusing to say anything else, hoping she would get the hint and talk about something else.

"I was thinking," she said after a brief moment of awkward silence. And how many intense conversations happened between men and women that started with a woman saying, "I was thinking"? And hearing no response from me, she proceeded to tell me exactly what she was thinking.

"I know the funeral is Saturday and I was wondering if you would like to drive down together. I can't fly because I have meetings on Friday, and I don't know long they will last. They will probably run right up until the time before we leave."

All sleep left my senses, and in a flash, I was fully alert! My ex-wife just asked me to drive to Virginia with her the day before the funeral, a twelve-hour car ride in the dead of winter, in a car, alone, for twelve hours of her having the opportunity

11

to tell me why we crashed on the rocks of matrimony and how it was all my fault. Hearing nothing from me while I thought about the request and trying to quickly weigh the pros and cons, she broke the silence again.

"Well, what do you think about the idea? Actually, you would be doing me a big favor because that's the only way I can go."

I was still processing mentally, mainly only hearing the words *ex-wife* and *road trip*. The rest of her words sounded like mumbo jumbo nonspeech of adults in a Charlie Brown cartoon.

When I finally refocused, I realized that we had entered another one of those awkward silences in the conversation. So to not be a complete ass, especially to someone that I had known for a significant part of my adult life, my little mind guy said, "Ask her what her husband thinks about the two of you traveling together all day and through a part of the night." Yeah, that was good so that's what I said. The words were out, and before me and my mind guy could pat ourselves on the back for thinking quick on our toes, Andrea seemed to have anticipated that question and said almost before I could finish the sentence it wasn't even an issue and her husband was fine with the whole thing. The quick response deflated us both as she continued to talk about how much he trusted her and that their marriage was rock-hard, rock-steady, or something like that cause my mind drifted off and I was half listening again after she said it wasn't a problem.

That wuss, I thought. I had only a few encounters with Andrea's husband and his niceness was damn annoying, walking round on this earth trying to be somebody! The man had never done anything to me, but I just disliked him on general principle! *Think! Think! Think! Nothing!*

After coming up with no reasonable response, I finally said, "OK."

"Great!" she screamed through the phone. Or maybe that was just how it sounded to me.

"I'll be there around ten in the morning on that day cause our meeting starts at 7:30." The excitement in her voice sounded like the enthusiasm a person would have anticipating spending time with a long-lost friend, even though we talked several times a year and I had just talked to her not too long ago about Lisa's passing.

To me I was still hearing Charlie Brown's teacher say, *"Wonk, wonk, wonk."* And how in the hell did she know the funeral was on Saturday?

"This should be interesting, and the trip will give us time to catch up," she continued. She seemed genuinely pleased that we were taking this trip together, even if the occasion was anything but pleasant.

"I know this is hard on you, Thomas, but if there is anything you need right now, just let me know. I'll send some flowers from both of us."

Again, all I could say was "OK." I didn't have the energy to debate the merits of this upcoming traveling road show. Andrea was in her element when it came to taking care of the details of doing what was appropriate in these types of situations, and I had no doubt the arrangement would be large, beautiful, and very expensive.

"I'll see you Friday morning, and you take care of yourself," she said, and then she hung up. Usually, she would have stayed on the line to make small talk, but I sensed that she knew I wasn't crazy about the trip, and she didn't want to risk me thinking of a reason it shouldn't happen.

If I had gotten my ass up and was functioning like a normal person, my mind wouldn't have been so slow, my mental guy so freaking uncreative. What does your husband think? That was all he had. Sometimes I wish I could fire his uncreative ass and get me a new mental mind guy who gave me big, bold, creative thoughts that allowed me to say the right things at the right time, the kind of thoughts that ended conversations with others cause there was no reasonable comeback, but I had him and his responses always had me saying stuff I should have kept in my head and then coming up with good comebacks after a situation was over, and I mean days after a conversation had ended. But in the end, I accepted that we all do the best that we can, and he was basically all I had for the rest of my life! Not to mention the fact that I'm literally talking to myself about myself.

So I had three days to pull myself together. I sincerely didn't want to go and dreaded the whole experience: the crying, the flowers, the black clothes, and all those conversations about being in a better place. I hated funerals. Just thinking about that whole experience started the tears again. So many feelings, regrets, and the agonizing sense of loss, all stuff that I was poorly able to deal with so I didn't. Something deep inside of me said that I needed to talk to someone because I was struggling desperately. Lisa was my rock, the one woman who made sense to me, and just knowing that she was there gave me strength to keep growing and to be me. Just knowing that she was a phone call away, that reassuring voice that told me when I was being ridiculous, that one person that kept me grounded most of my adult life, that beautiful face that greeted me when I arrived at college and walked me through that phase of my life and beyond. Because she was always there, I took her presence and support for granted. She helped me make sense of women and life and I loved her for it. And in a flash, she was gone forever!

I didn't want to go back to Virginia for that day, back to that personal hell, and for the first time in my life, I didn't have a clue as to what I should do next. I got out of my chair, walked into the kitchen, made myself a peanut butter sandwich, and washed it down with almond milk right out of the cartoon. I decided that I just needed to shake this off and get back into my life routines, that I would focus my thoughts on the present moment and get back to being more engaged in life. Yes! That was what I needed to do. I would go to the gym, get my energy level up, and then go to the store and buy some decent food, get back out into the world moving around. The idea of getting moving gave me a brief moment of hope, but before I could even make it to the bedroom, the overwhelming sadness started the waterworks again and I found myself on the bedroom floor, once again loss in my grief and crying like a lost child in the mall missing their mother.

This journey called life is rarely taken alone. Others have the unique ability to help us rise and discover the best we have to offer, or they may tear us down and leave us in an unfulfilled, constantly frustrated experience. However, the choice is always ours to make as we decide which path will we choose to take.

Thursday was a little better. I sat in my football chair, watching reruns of the Georgia versus Michigan football playoff game, one I watched no less than twenty times, and I watched it every time as if I were seeing it for the first time, always noticing some new wrinkles or a play that I had missed earlier. When that game ended, I had five others recorded and queued up. Running out of food, I found the strength to make one trip to the grocery store, where I bought food that could be nuked in the microwave and eaten in about two minutes, the kind of stuff all the experts say to stay away from. My buggy had been one big, processed food smorgasbord, yet the routine of shopping made me feel a little better. I had gotten up and out in the a.m. after spending the last few days in isolated purgatory. My grief at least on this day had morphed into an unfamiliar mental numbness, and I finally found the energy to venture out of my apartment.

It was cold but no clouds could be seen, and the sunny day gave the illusion of warmth. The sunshine on my face as I walked outside made me feel alive again. I felt a sense of accomplishment for getting out that morning. Now sitting in my chair, I was content as I watched my game as if I didn't know that Georgia would beat the brake shoes off of Michigan, who was completely overmatched against a bigger, stronger, and faster team. My cell phone started to vibrate as it sat on my little end table next to my chair. I had changed the settings after the last conversation with my ex and was pleased with myself for remembering to do so and pleased with the relief from the annoying ringing. An unfamiliar number with a Virginia area code flashed on the screen and I hesitated before finally answering it, believing that it was one of those random sales calls that can no longer be identified by the familiar 800 phone prefix.

"Hello," I said suspiciously, ready to hand up as soon as the sales pitch started or that guy from the police fund started asking for Johnny, his lame way of trying to avoid the immediate *click-click*.

"Hey Thomas, this is Bill," he said in a voice resonating nothing but defeat. Of all the people, I was surprised until I wasn't.

"Hey man, how you doing?" I asked out of respect and with as much sincerity as I could fake. I already knew the answer to that question cause the last time I saw Bill they were practically carrying him out of the hospital. He was literally screaming in grief! The scene would be

almost terrifying if it wasn't so sad, and
if I didn't know the source of his pain.
I didn't really know Bill, but I knew that
Lisa completed him in some way that made
him whole as a man, and I knew he would
never really recover, and that thought
made me sad for Lisa's daughter.

"As well as I can," Bill responded dryly.
Then there was silence as he waited for
me to say something, and frankly, I had no
idea what to say since Bill had called me
and I had said everything I felt I needed
to say.

Finally, I said, "Bill, what's up?" My
words seemed to break him from a trance,
like he had lost his train of thought right
after he had made the call. We were not
friends or old college buddies, and all
of our conversations were polite banter
that occurred when I saw him during
visits in Virginia or saw him during their
occasional trips to Michigan. Bill wasn't
into football so that wiped out a whole
category of mindless conversation that
would have happened on our infrequent
encounters.

"I wanted to know if you would be
willing to speak at the funeral," Bill
said, obviously assuming that I was going
to show up. If only Bill knew that I didn't
even want to make an appearance and was
actively contemplating some way of getting
out of going with Andrea.

I found myself saying, "Sure."

"I know Lisa would have liked that," he said.

"Yeah, I think you're right," I responded.

"Thanks, man. I'll text you the details."

Then he hung up. No "Bye," "I'll see you in a few days," or "Take care." He just hung up. And that was fine with me. Besides, what details are there other than a church location, a start time that won't matter cause black funerals never start on time anyway, and a date, which I already knew because his sister told me before I left Virginia? So whatever fantasy I had about not going was officially over. I knew he was right and that Lisa would have wanted me to be there and to say something. We had too much history for me not to honor the request, especially since I felt like I had failed her so many times in life. His call threatened my current state of numbness, and I thought I would break down, but I didn't, but the tears flowed softly down my face as I contemplated what a return would mean and having to speak at the funeral.

My little mental guy said, "Hey, don't you think you should think about what you were going to say?" But I ignored him and told myself that I would wing it because I didn't want to run the risk of another emotional setback. Besides he wouldn't give me anything decent to say right now anyway. His mediocre ass didn't help out with Andrea, so I had my doubts about his handiwork.

"What does your husband think?" Yeah right, a really brilliant comeback. Thoughts of Lisa could not be disconnected from thoughts of Lisa, and those very feelings were the source and instigator of my current state of mind. I looked back at the game. Confetti was falling and Georgia's coach was receiving a trophy on a makeshift stage surrounded by young, athletic male faces all smiling and grinning into the TV camera. "My dawgs did it again," I said to myself and then flipped off that game and went to the Georgia versus TCU matchup.

When we have lost our way, sometimes it's the simple things that we do each day that can remind us of who we are and where we should be.

Later that day was a little better and I was more hopeful that I could control my grief and the tears. I finally decided that I would just force myself to go to the gym, that I needed to do something to counteract the artery clogging food I had been eating for the past several days. If I really wanted to be fit, I would walk to the gym, seeing as it was only a half hour walk from my apartment complex, but like every other red-blooded American, I hauled myself around in my ozone-polluting car on trips that I and the environment would have been better served by me walking. I justified the drive by saying the neighborhood closest to the gym was a little sketchy and that it was too cold to walk, but the truth was I was just lazy and unmotivated for such a pedestrian journey. The gym near me was one of those discounted purple and gold places, the land of black spandex and expensive running shoes. For such a large facility, it always seemed too empty for its size. My old one near my house, when I was married to Andrea, was packed and a person had to wait to use some of the machines. You could shoot a cannon in this current gym and not hit a single soul.

I was greeted with a perfunctory hello from staff before they scanned my phone to make sure I was current on my auto pay; at least that's what I believed. As soon as I passed the counter, I headed straight for the weight machines, located at the center of the huge building. I didn't go to the men's locker room, and I almost never stretched before I worked out. Unlike serious workout gym rats, I dispensed with the preworkout routines and went right to work. I found the bicep curl machine, sat down, and went at it. From there I did the entire circuit in about twenty-five minutes. Exercising gave me a good way to focus my mind and keep me doing something I felt good about. It was a very effective distraction. After the weights, I headed over to the treadmill for a forty-minute walk and to start my people-watching.

I scanned the gym to observe all the interactions and movements that went on in the halls of fitness and for those interesting folk lost in their dedication and fantasies of physical prowess. Usually there was at least one guy with a too small tank top working out right next to the mirrors. More posing occurred than working out, and I always wondered if the ripped body was a product of hard work or medication. The truly dedicated didn't spend so much time staring at themselves in the wall of mirrors as they worked out.

Then there was the cover girl, wearing form-fitting tights and the matching form-fitting top, all complemented by colorful, expensive running shoes worn more for style than athleticism. Her sole goal was to be seen and look good and to not break a sweat. She worked out slowly, stopping to read messages on the phone, and constantly held up equipment use by taking way too long to work through her routine, but she didn't really care about anyone waiting because she was the cover girl. We should all feel blessed for her allowing us to gaze upon her beauty.

Then there were the regular Joes like me, people who came to try to improve their health, those who weren't concerned about being seen or whether their clothes matched but were just there to get some time in the gym to stave off or slow down all the unhealthy habits and the brutal process of aging. For us our goal was simple: to get in and do what needed to be done and get out as quickly as possible, and the everyday Joes came in all different shapes and sizes.

At this particular gym was one guy who worked out near the free weights. I noticed him every time. He stayed to himself and followed his own routine that looked more like a dance than a workout. He used small hand weights and wore headphones that I assumed piped in music so that he could maintain his rhythm. He wasn't a small man, but he wasn't significantly overweight either. He bounced and moved back and forth and side to side, all the while moving his arms and legs in tandem. He was always covered in sweat, and he maintained that same routine the entire time he was at the gym. And it was at that point that I realized that I had never seen him in the locker room, the few times I actually went in there myself to use the men's room. I never passed him in the parking lot, and I never saw him use any other equipment in the fitness center. Every time I saw him, he was dancing, and for such a big man, he was very light on his feet. The fact that I never saw him rest, never saw him leave or arrive, never saw him do anything other than dance made him seem mysterious and less real. He was always alone and never talked to anyone that I ever saw. Maybe my current struggles mentally with loss created this surreal image of him but I didn't care. I found a strange comfort in thinking that he just appeared and danced uninterrupted, lost in his own, undisturbed world.

After watching him for another fifteen minutes to see if he would do anything but dance, my attention drifted back to the parade of hanging TVs in the center. Besides, if I stared any longer, it would probably start to get creepy. So for that last part of my fitness regimen, I watched part of a sixty-minute repeat of a college game between Ohio State and Michigan State. When I left, the game was in the

27

third quarter, and I never understood why exercise facilities had such a horrible cable. They had thirty or so TVs and I could only find one interesting program per center!

When I finally left the treadmill and headed toward the door, I looked back to see if the dancer was still dancing, and he was, and I couldn't help but to smile as I exited the building to a "Thank you for coming and have a good day" from one of the staff behind the main counter. I felt better in that moment, better than I had felt in several days.

If we could only master the
virtue of patience, we would open
ourselves up a whole new collection
of life-affirming experiences.

Now the dreaded day had arrived. It was Friday morning and this day started better than some of my previous ones. I managed to get six hours of sleep and was feeling better, feeling a little more positive than I had been. But I also felt very anxious. I was tired of crying but knew I couldn't control the underlying emotions that produced the tears. Too many times when I thought I had gotten to a better place I would lose emotional control and break completely down, and I hated myself for it because it felt like weakness, it felt less manly, and I never liked crying men. And now I had become one. But today I was holding my emotions in check. I awoke early and made a real breakfast of scrambled eggs, wheat toast, and some low-sugar brand cereal.

I sat at my dinette table, and I found a quiet peace as I stared out the window. A bluebird had landed on the windowsill and was completely oblivious of my existence. It moved in that herky-jerky way that birds move, its tiny head bobbing quickly to the left and then to the right. It stretched its wings several times as it walked back and forth. I ate and watched this bird do what birds do. "I'll bet you never cried when one of your close bird friends died," I said to myself. Birds, like many other animals, did their life thing without emotion, without regret and any of the other myriad feelings and thought processes humans are subjected to. They don't worry about the past and are not anxious, worried, or even stressed about the future. They just live each day doing what their DNA has programmed them to do until they are eaten by some other animal, shot for sport, or just die of old age. The thought of a bird walking with a cane and chirping softly popped into my head. How amazing it would be if I could live like birds, just focusing on what was right in front of me, no constant processing of past events and discretions, no thoughts about an unknown future, no endless mind-numbing stream of thinking that even occurred in my sleep. I wondered about the pleasure and peace I probably could find by turning off the mental movies. Such thoughts felt like folly, but they provided me with a brief mental escape. And it was at that point that I was reminded how my body reacted to the thoughts produced in my head. Every one of them had the potential to cause a reaction, and if I could control the thoughts and be like the bird living in the moment, then I could find some sense of enduring peace. The bird finally looked my way, and I froze completely, convinced that if I moved, it would fly away. Then I found myself wondering what I looked like to a bird. And this is how the mind really worked, my mental guy working twenty-four/seven connecting thoughts and using them to conjure up other random, often useless ones just for the sake of keeping the ego happy and me existentially asleep. The head twitching stopped, the bird stared at me as if it were trying to look into my soul, or at least figure out if I was a threat to its life. Then as quickly as it had landed, it flew away and my morning entertainment ended.

I sat quietly trying not to think, watching the rising and falling of my chest as I breathed and felt the air enter and leave my body. And for a very brief moment, the mental movies ceased and there was an incredible stillness, a momentary peace, and then that damn mind guy showed up and the thought that there was stillness ruined the stillness! Goddamned! No rest for the mental weary. "She will be here soon, and you still need to pack," my mental mind guy said, and the camera turned back on and the mental movies starting rolling. So I got up from table, dumped the bowl into the sink, and headed into the room to pack because he was right this time, and that thought was useful.

Waiting, waiting, waiting. It was now eleven o'clock. Ten o'clock came and went and I was still in my apartment, mindlessly flipping through channels in an effort to find something interesting to watch, but to mainly kill time and control my frustration. Television was my best effort at meditation at that particular moment. And no word from my ex-wife. This was how our trip started: late!

Finally, around twelve o'clock, a message notice flashed on my phone. "Running late, we had a crisis in a plant in Wayne, be there as soon as I can." And there it was. Throughout our entire marriage, I had received many of this type of message. Something was always a crisis; something was always demanding her immediate attention and threatened the existence of a company that was more than a hundred years old. This was nothing new and was why I never wanted to work for the corporate "man"—because they owned your ass and everything in life took a backseat. The truth is we all work for some man or woman who controls our work and in many instances our leisure hours. Only the superrich wielded absolute control of every waking hour of the day. Yet I found some comfort in my life choices as the government "man" who I worked for rarely interfered with my leisure and leave time. I wasn't off of the treadmill of life, but at least I controlled my breaks. So seeing as how we were not leaving anytime soon, I decided to run out and get something to eat and if she came when I was out, then she would just have to wait, just like I had been waiting all morning!

As more time passed, I felt anxiety rising in me. "Be the bird. Be the bird. Be the bird," I kept telling myself as I left the parking lot heading to Wong's Palace to get some shrimp fried rice for lunch. But I didn't have the discipline, and the combination of anxiousness and frustration added to my current misery.

When I returned and pulled into my favorite parking space that happened to be available, the short trip managed to temporarily calm my frazzled nerves. I climbed out of the car and scanned the parking lot, no ex-wife to be seen anywhere. Damn! Damn! Damn! Damn! Damn! It was now well after 1 p.m., and I was still in Michigan. While I resolved myself to the reality that the trip was inevitable and that as much as I fantasized about not going, I knew deep down that the fantasy was just that: whimsical thoughts born out of anxiety and fear. But once I crossed the acceptance threshold, I was ready to leave on time and she still wasn't here!

As frustration creeped over into anger, I tried to remember my letting go YouTube videos as I realized that I was getting really upset about a situation that I had no control over and all I could do was wait, find something to do to kill the time, and just calm down.

The day rolled into early evening, and the evening rolled into night.

My frustration, impatience, and anger wearily melted into acceptance. And when she finally showed up, I was sitting in my favorite football chair eating one of those instant fifteen-minute pizzas I had found in the bottom of my refrigerator. The text notification flashed on my phone. Indifferently, I leaned over and read it while I ate.

Every journey always begins with
the idea that something needs
to happen, then we find ourselves
traveling someplace different
from where we started.

It was very dark when the black Navigator pulled into my apartment parking lot. She actually texted me the name of her car that she had arrived in and was waiting in the parking lot. A Navigator seemed a little odd since she worked for General Motors and was driving a car made by Ford, and why she texted the name seemed a bit much since I would notice the car she was sitting in when I got to the parking lot so I didn't need a name in the text, but that was my ex—over the top as usual. So I figured she must be driving her husband's car. I made a mental note to ask her about that one. I had been waiting for several hours and was mindlessly watching a replay of *Boomerang,* with Eddie Murphy and that skinny little woman with the big hair when Andrea finally arrived. We were supposed to have left early that morning but now it was dark. "I knew I should have found me a cheap flight out this morning," I said to myself, and I would already be there, spending time with my sister and her family. But I let Andrea Fullwood, the car executive, talk my ass into driving to Norfolk. "We can catch up and it will be fun," she said on that phone call that I should have ignored. I knew we would eventually talk about the "old times" at some point down that road, and as I remember, some of those old times needed to stay just that: old times and in the past. My mind guy told me to stop whining because I knew there was no way I would get a cheap flight flying out on the same day and I didn't have enough credit on any of my cards to even buy a same-day flight ticket anyway. But I ignored him and held on to the notion that I should have found another way to travel, one that involved just me. I then found myself wondering if that Trailways bus service was still operating.

Andrea and I had taken different paths in life after the divorce, and I was convinced that we would have conversations about all of it. We had talked briefly over the last six months but never in any real detail. Twelve hours in a car was a lot of time to talk about a whole bunch of details. I sat a little longer, not moving with any urgency, and my movie had just gotten to that Bang, Bang, Bang Thanksgiving dinner scene, which was one of my favorite scenes in the whole movie. Even though I had seen it too many times to count, it always made me laugh.

When I finally got up, grabbing my bag and heading to the door, I realized that most of the trip would now be through the night and that made the whole situation all that more depressing. I slowly closed and locked my door behind me and headed downstairs. My neighbor was standing in her doorway directly across from me while I was locking mine. She was wearing something close to nothing, and her shear onesie was revealing more than I really wanted to see. She smiled and waved when she saw me as she was standing there smoking a cigarette, in a smoke-free building. She didn't give a rat's ass about the smoking policy because she was supposed to be outside and at least ten feet from the entrance! And why was she standing at her door with her rule violating cigarette? My mind jumped from one question to another, and my conclusion was that I needed to stop being so incredibly cheap and find a decent apartment, one where half-naked, chunky women didn't stand in the hall at night smoking. This one was apparently attracting folk who don't really follow rules, and I wondered about other rules she was inclined to boycott and ignore. At least once a week she would wake me up in the middle of the night because I could hear her yelling and cursing with somebody, and then everything would go quiet again. The damn woman was a freak! So I nodded in response to her wave to be polite as I turned and headed downstairs. As I descended the stairs some of my questions were answered as I passed a big, burly man coming through the door. She must have just buzzed him in. "Booty call," I said to no one in particular, and I thought I said it low enough, but he obviously heard me and laughed.

As soon I got out the downstairs exit door, the cold air hit me right in the face and gave me instant chills. Driving in the winter in Michigan was bad enough, but driving at night was even worse. People froze from exposure in Michigan. The news had just talked about a student who got locked out of a dorm and froze at night. And now I was embarking on a twelve-hour drive in the middle of the night in the dead of winter in fifteen-degree weather with my ex-wife.

The big SUV was stopped parallel to the parking spaces closest to the building. The huge SUV made my car look like a matchbox toy. I really needed to change some things in my life, I thought as I hurriedly climbed into the Navigator. Perched on the thick, beige, leather passenger side seat, I couldn't help but to admire the splendor of this big SUV. It was about as plush as anything I had ever been in.

"Hey, we are finally off," she said. As if we had been delayed by minutes instead of hours. Her face wore that cheap defensive smile people wore when they knew that had messed up.

I wanted to complain and fuss but realized that it was just too late in the night, and it was all futile anyway. My positive affirmation videos said to stay positive and, in my effort to be better, I was trying. Besides, Andrea wouldn't have cared in the slightest. She would have said something like "I did the best I could, the meeting could not have been avoided, and we are here now so let's make the most of it." She was no longer my wife. There was nothing to do about the late start at this point anyway, and I just didn't have the energy for anything but riding in peace and quiet. We already had had enough fights when we were married to last two lifetimes. Andrea has always been a fighter, and if I started a "You are ridiculously late" fight, she would not hesitate to go toe-to-toe and it was just too damn cold, it was too damn dark, and I was too damn tired for such a rocky start to such a long trip. So I slapped some lipstick on this pig of a start and tried to smile as I made myself comfortable. She then gave me an inquisitive look and I figured my smile was coming off as disingenuous and forced, and I remembered how hard it was to fool someone who knows you intimately, especially a perceptive ex-wife.

The large vehicle moved easily out of the parking lot, and we headed toward Telegraph Road. We drove south until we got to Interstate 75. Once we hit Interstate 75, Andrea gunned the big SUV and it smoothly accelerated to a cruising speed of seventy-five miles per hour. The one thing I felt positive about was our ability to make good time on this trip since the night drive meant significantly less traffic. I prayed we wouldn't hit snow because driving in the snow at night was an experience out of a *Twilight Zone* episode. Heavy night snow meant limited visibility and a lot of cars and trucks in ditches. I wanted to ask Andrea if she had her winter emergency kit but was too afraid to hear the answer if she didn't because I would worry all the way to Virginia. I told myself that she packed a blanket, candles, matches or a lighter, snacks, and water. The best winter travelers carried flares too for emergencies.

"I'm sorry for the late start, Thomas, but I really thought the meeting would be short, but we found some serious issues with the accounting reports, blah blah blah," she said once we were out on the interstate and headed to Toledo.

I appreciated her effort to explain, but I didn't really care because that was all behind us now. "Stuff happens," I responded. She knew me well enough to know that short responses meant that I was annoyed and didn't want to talk. That's why I believe she was waiting all the way until we got out onto the main freeway before she said anything. After that effort, she gave up talking and we rode in silence. I decided to try to get a quick nap early so I would be awake during those tough two o'clock to 5 o'clock driving hours.

As I looked around at the interior, everything dripped of luxury. The truck had heated and cooling seats and even a seat massage feature! If you have to travel long distances in the middle of the night, this was definitely how to do it in style and comfort. I set the seat warmer to low, reclined as far back as I could, and turned on the massage feature. Andrea looked over at me as if she wanted to say something. She opened her mouth to speak, but before any words came out, she closed it and looked at the road ahead. I was wrapped in the cocoon of expensive leather, plush and warm padding, and a soothing vibration from the massage feature buried deep into the lumbar part of the seat. This chair felt like a recliner on wheels: an impressive, expensive traveling comfort that allowed me to slip easily into the peace found only in sleep.

Traveling long distances can be a test of one's patience. If we learn to see the traveling as the real experience, then we have eliminated the wasteful act of impatience and have learned to enjoy every mile traveled.

I was leaning toward the window when I finally awoke. I casually looked down at my watch and noticed that we had been traveling for only a couple of hours. Based on that travel time, we were barely in Ohio and had most of the trip in front of us. Endless miles of turnpikes in Ohio and Pennsylvania and meandering highways in Maryland and northern Virginia waited for us in the darkness.

My mind came online slowly as I shook off my restless nap, and the first thing I noticed was that we were not moving. I looked out the window with a greater since of urgency and noticed that we were at a rest stop on the Ohio turnpike. The lot was empty except for two cars parked close to the sidewalk leading to the main building. *Bathroom break,* I thought as I moved to sit more upright in the seat, and then I noticed a light snoring sound coming from the driver's side of the SUV as Andrea was leaning against the driver's side window. The engine idled easily and kept the big truck warm and cozy. This is the kind of crap that drove me crazy! Two people traveling, and we were only

two hours into the trip but sitting at
some strange rest stop and sleeping in
an idling car! My overactive imagination
kicked in and started to spend all kinds
of crazy scenarios with creepy-looking
Freddy Krueger characters walking up
to the car and breaking the window. But
before I went too far down that rabbit
hole, I realized that I did need a
bathroom break and found myself hustling
quickly to open the door and then sliding
out of the car. When I was young, I had
much more control of my breaks, but as I
aged, I realized that much of that control
was gone and my body had decided that it
needed to relieve itself regardless of
whether I was in a restroom or not. I was
moving fast now and slammed the car door
as I left the vehicle.

Andrea popped straight up at the sound
of the closing door, startled out of her
peaceful rest stop sleep. She popped up
in a perfectly erect position, and it
was funny as hell. I took some comfort
in surprising her and laughed quietly
under my breath. Then I realized that God
didn't like ugly as the laughter seemed
to tell my bladder that it was time to
do its thing. I found myself sprinting
to beat the pee train that was about to
start without my consent or an available
restroom latrine. I made it just in time
as I crashed through the restroom door
and holding my pants in that way young
boys used to do for no apparent reason

other than the thought that they thought it looked cool.

As I strolled leisurely out of the rest stop building, I felt the extreme cold air that smacked me in the face. In my haste, I failed to get my coat and was paying the price now as the cold creeped through every orifice of my body just to remind me that I was not properly dressed, and it was cold as hell in the Midwest in December. My walk turned into a jog until I reached the door of the car. Getting back into the car was like climbing into some motorized cocoon of warmth.

Andrea looked over at me and smiled.

"You had to go pretty bad, huh?" she finally said with that mischievous smile smirk.

"What do you want me to say?" I responded.

Then she opened her door and leisurely got out. She was carrying her coat and put it on immediately as she closed the door and headed toward the building. I couldn't prove it, but I know she was laughing at my ass as she had the benefit of watching me running like a drunken monkey and holding my pants in the crotch area. I should have felt some kind of way about her laughing and us stopping unnecessarily, but all that seemed to go out the window as the embarrassment of my lack of bladder control basically ended any real opportunity to complain about the situation. *My trip from hell with my ex-wife,* I thought as I now sat alone looking out the front windshield into the darkness of the night. She still could have woken me up to drive while she slept and we could have been farther down the road, maybe in Pennsylvania by now. "You are absolutely right Thomas," the little man in my head told me, and I felt a little better because of his affirmation.

After a few minutes, I watched Andrea as she strolled back to the truck, walking in that easy la, la, la way that she moved, a motion that represented no sense of urgency and suggested that we had no place to be that required us to rush. Watching her made me wonder about the universe and karma and personal grace and protection. Andrea was one of those people where things always seemed to work out for her, with little stress or effort. Don't get me wrong. She had a big job, but it didn't seem to be so big that it stressed her, or if it did, I never saw it. She had that goofy nerdy husband who seemed built just for her quirky personality. Promotions and success flowed easily for her, even when she was married to me. There seemed to be people in the world who moved easily and effortlessly through life as their stars aligned to minimize the bumps and bruises of the ride. I know I was on the outside looking in and a person never really knows another person's life at that distance, but from my view, hers looked pretty damn sweet.

Andrea climbed back into the car and instantly looked at the gas gauge. "Let's get some gas before we get back on the road," she said.

"Yasser, Messer, and I's pump for you," I said in my best slave imitation as she backed the car out of the space and headed toward the gas pumps on the other side of the building.

"Funny man," she responded.

"It's your world and I'm just glad to be in it," I continued.

She paid for the gas directly at the pump and I got out, this time with my coat and pumped it.

Within minutes the big SUV was accelerating down the entrance ramp back onto the turnpike. I turned back toward the window, determined to go back to sleep, but this time sleep did not come so easily, and I found myself engaging in a story—well, really just listening and occasionally adding "OK," "That's interesting," and "Wow!" as Andrea talked about some trip she and what's-his-name went on to New Orleans and visited some cemeteries with alligators or something like that. Honestly, I was half listening but felt the need to support her during these tough driving hours.

Eventually, after a few hours of these vacation stories, my chivalry faded and

Rick Tenmoo

I found my escape on another trip to
the land of napville, leaning against
the passenger side door once again, arms
folded and the seat vibrating softly.

We don't always appreciate the full
value others bring into our lives.
Only by understanding who we really
are deep inside ourselves can we fully
appreciate the value of others.

This second time when I awoke, the big truck was parked at a gas pump; gas was the Achilles' heel of the big SUV, which was long on luxury and short on mileage. I debated whether I should help her pay for the gas and after some personal deliberation decided against it. I figured if she could afford the car, she could afford the gas. Then I found myself debating if I wanted to get out and weather the cold to go inside and buy something to drink. From what I could guess, we were well into Pennsylvania and close to the end of the turnpike. Also, I was a little bit surprised when Andrea didn't wake me up but figured she let me sleep to make up for the fact that we had to drive across the country like Smokey and the Bandit trying to get to Virginia in the wee hours of the night.

Suddenly Andrea appeared on the passenger side at the window. It seemed as if she had popped up out of nowhere and I almost jumped out of my seat! She laughed and told me to roll down the window.

"I paid for the gas. You going to pump it?"

"Sure."

She handed me two coffees through the passenger side window. Damn, I had to get out anyway. I grabbed my coat off the back seat and pulled my skullcap from the door pocket. Standing outside, it felt like the temperature had dropped another ten degrees since our last stop in Ohio.

"I only use premium!" she yelled from inside the car.

"Of course," I replied. I didn't know how much gas we had when we stopped, but when the pump finally shut off, the cost was $95 and eighteen gallons. Ain't no way I could afford to put gas in this rolling mini hotel on wheels. *Thank God for my gas-sipping Sonic,* I thought.

Within seconds of getting back into the Navigator, we were ready to get back on the freeway for another few hundred miles or so before the thirsty truck needed another refresh.

"You read my mind. I was thinking about getting something to drink just before you sneaked up on me and scared the crap outta me."

"I wasn't trying to scare you. I was just making sure you were going to pump the gas because if you were too tired, I wouldn't have to get back out of the car to pump," she responded matter-of-factly.

"At any rate, you enjoyed that a little too much. You know that's how women get smacked, surprising men and then *bam!*

Whacked upside of the head out of sheer reflex."

"You looked more like you were trying to move away than trying to hit."

"That's cause at the last minute before I went into defense mode, I realized it was you," I said, realizing that the last comment was so unbelievable we both started laughing.

"Where are we?" I asked.

"About an hour past Harrisburg, we should be close to the Maryland state line."

"I'll pay the tolls." I said this like it was a big deal. I figured that she knew my cheap ass would take the cheaper option, but I knew deep down that she really didn't care. People with her kind of money would not sweat a few dollars or less in tolls, and that included going and coming, but people on budgets like me would.

"OK, but you missed the ones in Ohio," she responded indifferently.

Our luck continued to hold, and no snow had shown up yet on this voyage through Big Ten country. We saw very few cars on the road, more semitrucks, and for some odd reason more RVs than I remember seeing during my yearly drive to Virginia. The ease that the Navigator moved down the highway was comforting and reassuring. I understood now at least one of the reasons folk bought such large SUVs.

"How's your family?" Andrea finally asked when the driving silence started to creep in.

"Everybody's good."

"Vett still in the Atlanta?"

"Yeah, I think that's where she'll retire."

"What's she doing these days?"

"Running a clothing and gift shop in one of those small towns outside of the ATL. She told me which one, but I forgot. You know that's her thing."

"I didn't know that. I always liked her."

"I know you did, and she liked you," I said cautiously.

"I'll bet your other sister didn't like me. I always felt like she was trying to figure me out every time I saw her. She was nice, but it was a cautious niceness."

"I don't know about that. We've always been close. If I liked someone, she was cool with them," I responded, wondering to myself where this conversation was going.

"Yeah, I know, and when you stopped liking someone, she did too."

"I don't know if I completely agree with that. You know sisters and moms are funny about sons and brothers. They just want to know that we ain't married to skanky women."

"I don't know," she said, and then she paused as if to seriously think about her next comment. "Did either of your sisters wonder why we didn't work out?"

And there it was. I had to admit I was impressed how she slid that question into our small talk about my family.

"Well, if they did, they didn't ask me because we don't normally get into each other's personal life, unless we're invited."

"How do you invite someone into your personal life?"

"By asking for advice."

"Oh."

"Yeah, we stay out of each other's personal life. I think it's because we all are just trying to deal with our own stuff, and out of respect we try to mind our business."

"If they had asked, what would you have said?"

My mind was working overtime and I had to get this part right. We had been divorced a long time, but I knew that women never let anything go and she probably still felt some kind of way about how our marriage ended and somehow it was my fault, my inability to deal with her success, my failure to accept my role as some kind of perverse alpha male pretending to be a beta. There's a part of me that knew deep down she would never fully understand my issues with our relationship and my expected role as the husband of a supersuccessful wife. My thoughts about our situation made me think of that old, dead, white guy singing that song about doing it his way!

Before I figured out what to say, I noticed headlights in the rearview mirror. The lights looked to be moving fast and were closing in on Andrea's SUV.

"You see that car coming up behind us?" I said.

Andrea hadn't noticed and looked up casually as the lights got brighter and brighter. At first, she thought I was stalling and trying to divert the conversation until she saw exactly what I saw.

"I see it now," she responded, looking intently at the rearview mirror and seeing the fast-approaching headlights.

"I know this fool is going to slow down," I said.

Before I even completed the sentence, the lights got even brighter and then they disappeared as the car or whatever kind of vehicle it was suddenly and without warning slammed into the back of the Navigator. The big SUV shook, and Andrea struggled to maintain control as the rear started to sway to the right and then back to the left in a zigzag pattern.

"Shit, shit, shit, shit" was all I could say.

I could hear the screeching sound of the tires as Andrea yanked the steering wheel to the right more out of reflect and then she mashed on the brakes. The tires seemed to scream even louder as they tried to grip the road and slow the big truck. The Navigator turned sideways, and then I felt it tilt as the wheels on the driver's side of the car left the ground. By that time both of us were screaming and cursing, and all I could think was that were going to flip and that we were going to die, broken and frozen on the highway, and that's what our dumb asses got for traveling in the dead of the night in two-degree weather when we should have been on the road during the day!

After what seemed like minutes but was actually seconds, the left tires hit the road again and the truck started to slow rapidly, and we finally came to a complete stop. We sat and stared at each other with looks that could only be described as complete and total terror. My heart was beating so rapidly I thought it was going to literally pop right out of my chest. The truck was stopped, but Andrea still had the brake pressed to the floor.

"We need to get out of the middle of the highway," I finally said after a long silence, but Andrea didn't move, and the truck was still in drive mode. She looked like a person frozen in time, and the only way I knew she was alive was the rapid rising and falling of her chest. So I slowly reached over, hand trembling wildly, and pressed the piano type of button with an *N* embossed on it. Instantly the engine shifted into idle.

"What the hell just happened?" she finally said after she came out of her terror trance.

My mind was a jumble of confusion as my breathing slowed. I realized that at some point during the last few seconds I had grabbed onto the grip above the passenger side door and my right hand was still tightly sneezing the hell out of it. My left hand was now in my lap, but it was still trembling. As the adrenaline rush subsided, I looked down slowly at my crotch, praying that my pants were still dry. Thank God for small miracles! In our confusion, we both had completely forgotten about the car that had hit us. Those headlights were still there, but they were partially visible as the car was now off to the left and about fifteen yards back.

"We need to get out of the middle of the road," Andrea said, as if I hadn't just said that exact thing a few seconds ago. Then she put the car in drive and slowly pulled over to the road shoulder. Her hands trembled as she maneuvered the truck off the highway, but I was glad to see that her mind was processing again, glad that no one was behind us and that no one hit us while we sat in the middle of the interstate.

The next thought that came into mind was about damage to the car. That little guy in my head said, "You all right. Go see how bad the damage is." That's what my mind was saying, but my body was still in terrified mode, hands still not steady, and my chest still rising and falling, albeit slightly slower by now.

After a few moments of just sitting and recovering from what had just happened, I finally said, "Leave the car running," as I slowly unbuckled my seatbelt and climbed out of the car, grabbing my coat from between the two back seats as I slid out into the cold air.

I still was reacting more than I was thinking, and like many men, I now was getting pissed that something had happened that scared the living crap outta me. When I got to the back of the car, I was expecting to see nothing but sheet metal carnage, but I saw a bumper that had been bent in a downward position, but it was still attached. The impact had pressed in a large portion of the face of the bumper. The dual exhaust tailpipes did not seem to be impacted as they continued to expel the engine exhaust that rose and escaped into the air.

Life is a process of letting go
of all the things we fear and
finding the courage to simply
accept what is, exactly as it
comes to us at each moment.

A feeling of relief came over me, and I knew that we would be able to keep going and eventually get out of this darkness, get out of this cold, miserable winter weather. My relief started to fade as my mind regained control and my automatic mental pilot switched off. The car that hit us was now moving, and it was creeping up behind us once again. I could feel the fear rising in my chest, and it reminded me that I was standing behind a running car with another unknown car slowly approaching and I had nothing to protect myself except hands whose sole goal was to stay warm in my coat pockets.

Before I could think of something to put me in a defensive position, the car was a few feet away and someone was climbing out. The driver was tall and Caucasian. He wore a blue and white plaid shirt, blue jeans, and heavy-looking brown boots. His hair was thick and black and covered most of his face, and for some reason I couldn't figure out, he didn't have on a coat. He looked like he was in his midforties.

I was still trying to get my mind in gear to do something, but nothing came to mind so I just stood there like an idiot as this strange man approached me. Finally! My mind woke the hell up and started thinking. *You can punch him and run if this thing goes sideways, jump into the truck, and haul ass. Watch his hands to see if he has a gun or knife.* My mind guy said, "Yeah, I know it's dark, dumbass, but look anyway. You may see a flash or reflection for the metal of a weapon or a sudden movement where he raises his hands quickly in an aggressive motion." Now I had a plan, and my mind was in full defense mode.

And just as I started to feel a little better, I heard the engine cut off. I thought, *That damn Andrea! Goddamned! There goes my escape plan. Now if two more hillbilly-looking white boys climb out of the back seat or passenger side of that car, I have to worry about her and me! If this confrontation goes sideways, I now have to fight with my bear hands or get ready to squeal like a pig! Hardhead ass woman. One more obvious reason why we didn't work. Don't listen for shit!* Then I heard the car door open and close and the footfalls approaching the rear of the truck. But to my good fortune and by the grace of God, no one else emerged from the car. It appeared that this man was traveling solo.

"You OK?" Andrea said, more telling me than asking as she reached the back of the car and saw me standing near the passenger

63

side rear taillight. I was trying to create some cover and use the car's edge to create some protection, but that effort was out the window because Andrea stood directly behind the truck two feet from the bumper. She was now completely exposed and standing almost directly in front of our late-night highway guest. I had no other choice but to get out from near the car and stand next to her.

"I hope you all are all OK, and I'm really sorry. I guess I was going too fast and wasn't paying attention," the man said in a tone barely above a whisper. To me his soft, whispery voice seemed out of character with his *Deliverance* persona. Something seemed off about his movements though. He moved like someone working way too hard to stay completely vertical. He was staring at me as he apologized because Andrea was looking at the damage to her car. He looked sincerely concerned and saddened by his lack of driving focus.

Having assessed the damage, Andrea finally looked up at the stranger and then at me. The stranger reached in his pocket, and out of reflex I stepped back. Andrea didn't bulge. She just stood there being a big, obvious target for anything to happen next. To my relief, he pulled out a wad of money big enough to choke two horses! He peeled off ten bills and attempted to hand them to me, but Andrea reached out and took the bills before they could reach my hand.

"Is that enough to take care of the damage?" he asked, not sure who was the most appropriate person to address. Andrea held the bills close to her face to counteract the darkness and counted the money quickly, using the light of the moon, and said yes.

Until this day I had no idea how much money he gave her because when I asked her later, she simply said, "Enough." So I guess that was none of my business because I didn't know how much "enough" converted into in real dollars.

He apologized again and wished us safe travels. Once the money exchanged hands, the man didn't turn and walk away. He backed slowly back to his car until he was parallel with the driver side door. He waved politely as he climbed back into his car. It was at that point that I realized that he was just as afraid of us as we were of him. The car turned and moved back out onto the highway. Once the man was back on the highway, he took off like a bat out of hell, driving as fast as he was before.

"I thought you were going to stay in the car," I said before I even realized I had said it.

"I had to come see what was going on and to check on you," she said, in that same old matter-of-factly way.

"What if he had been a crazy hillbilly? Then what?" I responded.

She looked at me with a dismissive smile and said, "You always think the worst of people."

"Famous last words of black folk lost in the woods and last seen talking to a hillbilly on side of the interstate in the middle of the night," I responded, slightly annoyed by the flippant way she dismissed the potential threat.

"Let's get outta here. It's too cold to be standing here, and we still have a long way to go," she responded as she turned and headed back to the front of the truck.

I stood there for another moment, allowing myself to calm down and to remind myself that this conversation didn't need to turn into a fight. I was still pissed off by how that whole situation went down. She should have stayed in the car and let me handle it and got out when he left. But that wasn't Andrea's way, and deep down she did exactly what I figured her hardhead ass would do.

Within seconds we were back on the road, wrapped in the warmth of the big truck and feeling safe and content and moving on down the road to our final destination.

This time I started the conversation. "So that was pretty messed up, right?

"Yeah, it was."

"Were you scared?"

"Yeah, when I thought we were dead when my truck tires came off the ground and I thought we were going to flip. They say your life flashes before your eyes, but all I could think about was dying."

"What about that weird white dude? I know that had to freak you out because it freaked the hell out of me."

"If I had thought about it long enough, it probably would have scared me too, but all I was thinking about was the damage to the truck."

"You know that whole situation could have gone sideways, and we would have had to deal with some serious stuff. And you walked almost right up to him when you got out."

"I wasn't thinking about that man, and I barely noticed him until I was standing in front of him, and you were there to back me up anyway."

"Back you up with what? If that guy had a gun, we would have been ass out of luck."

"That never even crossed my mind. I'm just glad he didn't do more damage than he did, and my baby is still good." She patted the dashboard as if she were patting the head of a puppy.

I wasn't sure how to react to her last comment. Too many people too many times not comprehending the seriousness of a dangerous situation. But I knew if that guy had a gun and if he was crazy, that we would have been screwed. She would have gone down first because she basically walked right up to the guy like he was some long-lost friend. Then I would have had to decide to try to fight or run and

67

running would have been the most viable option as the darkness would have provided excellent cover. The thought of running and leaving Andrea made me feel like a coward, but my mind kept telling me that there was no need for both of us to die. And besides, didn't I tell her oblivious ass to stay in the truck where she would have been safe and could have driven off? That thought made me feel a little better, and because sometimes you just can't save people from doing stupid stuff instead of being safe and careful. Most people are just sheep!

"Well, I'm glad it's over and we are back on the road. Hey, you got a gun?" I asked as I once again thought about what could have happened.

"You mean do I have a gun right now, in this car, or do I own a gun?"

"Both."

"No, I don't have a gun in this truck, and yes *we* have guns in our house. My husband likes to go to the range and has a collection of them in a gun vault in the basement."

"In the basement? So it didn't cross your mind to bring one on this trip because we were traveling at night, in the cold, and anything could happen?"

"No, it didn't, and I personally don't like guns, have never shot a gun, and don't even like the idea of guns, but I let him have his because he keeps them locked away and I never see them or have to touch them."

I didn't know what the "idea" of guns was all about but decided to let that remark go.

"If somebody breaks into your house, you have to go down into the basement, unlock the gun vault, pick a gun, and then load the gun and then go back upstairs and confront some robber."

"Nobody's breaking into our house. You've seen our neighborhood, Thomas. We don't have a house-break-in kind of address."

"What's a break-in kind of address? Crime is everywhere and anything can happen everywhere."

"That's your opinion because you have an overactive imagination. Certain neighborhoods have more crime than others, and some have virtually no crime. It's a fact. The more expensive the zip code, the less crime and the more responsive the police. That's just how it works, and you should know this because you worked in planning, and you saw crime stats."

Hot damn! Now my ex was schooling me about neighborhood crime, crime statistics, and city planning. "Not sure if that's 100 percent correct, but I get your point. Just saying no neighborhood is completely immune from crime."

"But the numbers are a lot better for some than others."

"Come on now. I know that white dude freaked you out a little and didn't you find yourself wishing you had something more powerful than your bare hands or mine?"

"Honestly, my mind was so focused on my truck that I didn't even notice that guy until he was right in front of me. It was dark, and besides, I don't think the worst of people like you do."

"The worst of people? This is a strange dude that just drove into the back of your truck in the middle of the night, and we are the only people on the road and you saying I think the worst of people? You sound like a crazy person. Anybody else would have been cautious as hell and would have tried to find something in the car for defense before they confronted that guy, but you didn't have jack squat in your car for protection and I had to get out with nothing but a prayer and a hope."

"Thomas, people don't jack people like you and me. One look at this truck and they know that if something happened to us, there are people that would raise holy hell."

"Again, there goes that crazy Andrea talking. Even if that was remotely true, that reaction that those people would have would be after the fact, Andrea. After we didn't show up in Virginia, after someone files a missing person's report, and after the lazy ass police in this area gave a good Goddamn and started to look for us. We would be long gone."

"No, we wouldn't cause they only mess with people they think no one cares about."

"Do you honestly believe that?"

"It's the truth."

"Your truth maybe, but I still wish you had one of those guns from that vault in this car."

"You think too much about too much stuff that never happens. That's your problem, and it keeps you from becoming and doing more in life."

"Because I think we should have a gun at night while driving twelve hours in the dead of winter and we just had a potentially near-death experience with a strange random white dude, you think I have a problem of overthinking and it's affecting my life choices?" The old Thomas would have been going off right now, yelling and screaming at the insult that was just given.

The whole conversation was now starting to feel like de ja vu. We had had too many of these types of conversations where at the end of the day my thoughts were somehow linked to some deficiency in my character. But this time I dialed it back. I took a deep breath like my YouTube videos taught me to, exhaled, and forced myself to relax.

The rising anger and frustration subsided. I calmed down enough not to curse her ass out, and I remembered again that Andrea was no longer my wife or my problem. She was just butt naked wrong, but she could never be convinced of her wrongness, and at this stage in our lives, it just

71

didn't matter anymore. She was firmly in the friend zone, and I frankly didn't give a rat's ass what she thought of me anymore.

The very realization of our current relationship made me feel a little better and reminded me that I just needed to ignore her big bourgeois, self-righteous personality. I really liked my current narrative and felt no need to defend it. I had time to travel and to visit family, time to think and wonder and to simply do anything, and I loved that reality that I saved so much of my time for me and the things that I found important. I loved the amount of control I refused to sell on the open market. I also knew that Andrea never really understood or appreciated my life's philosophy, and I used to think that it fed some of the resentment she felt for me toward the end of our marriage. She saw it as weakness while I saw it as strength. We both came from places where wealth was not present, hers more severe than mine, but I had a strong, close-knit family that always supported me, and I knew who I was regardless of how society tried to define me. Andrea always had something to prove, and she developed the skills to match her innate intelligence and bought into the proverbial American dream, hook, line, and big house on the hill. She never questioned life's standards of success, and I never accepted them.

The last few minutes and the lateness of the night were starting to take their toll, and I could feel the weariness in my body as I again fought the desire to sleep. The physical fatigue of traveling and the movement of the truck all worked in tandem to create the perfect sleeping conditions. I didn't feel the need to talk anymore, but I did want to stay awake to make sure Andrea stayed up too and that we wouldn't wind up on the side of the road parked and sleeping again. But in the end, I knew staying up was a losing battle for me and that I had to trust that Andrea would stay awake and not crash and kill us both.

"Are you OK?" she asked as she glanced at me out of the corner of her eyes.

I guess my silence caused her to ask. But there was nothing left to say. It was dark, we almost died, and we still had at least six more hours to go before we arrived in Norfolk.

"I'm fine," I heard myself saying as I leaned into the passenger side window once again, making myself more comfortable.

I looked out and stared into the darkness. Ghostly wooded areas raced past as we moved quickly down the highway. Traveling at night always had a surreal effect on me. I felt the reassuring movement of the SUV, but the world seemed to disappear and lose its place in my mind. My last thought before I fell asleep was wondering how the astronauts felt moving through empty space as they traveled to the moon.

Once off on a journey, you inevitably reach a point of no return, where it makes more sense to keep going than to turn around.

Snow started to fall lightly as we moved through Maryland and closed in on the DC metro area. I slept in fits and spurts and Andrea played her music tunes from her synced phone to keep her awake and driving. When I wasn't sleeping, I stared out the window watching the world pass me by, trying not to think about why we were traveling and where we were going. It was late, but we would be out of the darkness soon and back into a world filled with sunshine.

The darkness made me think about how many of the earthly processes we never think about. The rising and setting of the sun, the warmth provided, and the processes that create food to eat. Our planet provided everything we needed to be who we are, and most days we took all of those gifts for granted without so much as an afterthought. I then tried to imagine a world with no sun but found that line of wondering way too terrifying, but I had to admit that it did make me feel grateful, even for the current darkness. Landscapes illuminated by moonlight passed as if they were on parade; a silhouette or an actual cow or horse standing in an open field, a moonlit menagerie of urban, suburban, and rural life floated by as if it all existed for my personal amusement. I found this aspect of traveling to be restorative.

My mind wondered about things beyond people and relationships and played in the metaphysical world beyond culture. The darkness and the feeling of being a quiet observer moving through time with nothing more to do than to just keep moving, seeing, and experiencing. When I wasn't lost in my metaphysical traveling experiences, I occasionally thought about Lisa regardless of how hard I tried not to. The reality that we were tracking ever so slowly back to Virginia made not thinking about her impossible for my undisciplined mind. The thoughts rose as pictures in my head, full of all of the detail, color, sound, and beauty of any movie I ever saw in a theater. My mind wondered and the memories randomly played, my ego's way of connecting all experiences to reinforce the perception of control.

I found myself lost in another memory of Lisa and the moments we shared with each other and others.

Our memories are not always as accurate as we want to believe. And when we forget, our minds fill in the empty spaces with inaccurate information that becomes our new truth.

I arrived at church late after leaving a night class at NSU. I arrived at the church at seven fifteen. As I approached the stairs, I saw Lisa and Bill standing on the top landing right in front of the main entrance. She was laughing at something Bill had said, and he was smiling back at her with that creepy old man smile. Well maybe it was just a regular, run-of-the-mill smile and I now thought it was creepy because I knew the rest of the story.

"You're late," she said to me as I climbed the stairs.

"Have they started yet?" I responded.

"No," Bill said, inserting himself into the conversation.

"Then I'm right on time," I said as I passed the couple and entered the church.

Lisa grabbed my hand as I passed and smiled at me. She casually let it go as I moved into the building. I stopped, looked back, blew her a kiss, and said, "And by the way, when is Henry coming back to town?" Bill looked annoyed with the comment, but Lisa looked unfazed.

"Next weekend," she responded in that easy way that women have when men try to trip them up. Henry Akan was Lisa's longtime boyfriend and was attending school at Savannah State College. He drove up every other weekend to see the love of his life, and to me they made a great couple. He adored the ground she walked on, and she loved him as well, or so I thought. Lisa gave Bill one of those old lady bodies-not-touching hugs and headed down the stairs. Bill followed me into the church because he was a part of the choir as well and I couldn't help but to wonder if she had talked him into joining as she had me.

My mind went back to the phone number on a piece of paper that I found on my windshield, and I decided that I would call it the next day. "Nothing but beautiful possibilities," I said to myself as I moved to take my spot in the choir stand, near the back behind the pulpit.

"What?" Bill responded.

"Oh, just thinking about something that happened earlier today," I said as I headed up the stairs where we practiced.

I remembered that whole day like I was watching it in replay, even the conversations. Well maybe not the actual verbatim words but the tone and the intent. That was the day I got the phone number that started the courtship that eventually led to a five-year relationship, a divorce, and eventually a friendship and a ride in the middle of the night to Norfolk. Sometimes we never know the roles people are ultimately destined to play in our lives. I then found myself wondering if that was also the beginning of the end for Lisa and Henry. After that day and over the course of the next year, I saw Henry less and less until he stopped coming to Norfolk State altogether. In retrospect, that day was a beginning for my relationship with Andrea, and during those years, I really believed that she and I were destined souls and we would be eternal, or at least until I croaked from one of those black man diseases. Riding with her now, I found myself wondering what could have been if we had the patience to keep trying. Then I thought about that last conversation, the near-death experience, and the conversation that followed, and that what-if thought faded as quickly as it had arisen.

During our drive when we talked about our early years, we realized that many of those experiences included Lisa, and that made those memories hard to recall, even in conversation. I thought of *The Color Purple* play and watching Lisa and Andrea dazzling a crowded campus theater with their acting skills. Lisa was Celie and Andrea was Miss Millie. We were all so young, healthy, fit, and just awesome. I was finally starting to understand the phrase that youth is wasted on the young. I was at least twenty-five years out of school and was starting to feel the beginning signs of getting older, feeling the occasional soreness and watching the expedited exodus of my hair. When I was lost in my own thoughts, I couldn't help but appreciate that Andrea and I were making this trip together. Our shared history of our young adult years was comforting. Aging has a way of putting past experiences into perspective, and many times they reveal to us what's most important in life when we are paying attention. Too many times we lose ourselves in the pettiness and unimportant aspects of living. My memories of Lisa and my youth were starting to sadden my already somber mood so I decided to engage Andrea in conversation as a diversion from thinking about other, more depressing things.

"Hey, so what's new with GM? Any new cars coming out that I should know about?" I hoped this question would lead to a long update on her job and her meteoric rise in the car company. She started laughing. I didn't know that I had made a joke, but it was good to hear her laugh.

"You know your cheap ass ain't buying a new car. Thomas, you know you don't buy new cars, just used ones. You remember when you borrowed a loaner SUV from me because you didn't want to spend money on a rental?"

"I remember," I said, but that wasn't the reason. I wanted to test drive that Tahoe so I could see if that was the truck for me. Once again, more laughter, and it was the loud, deep kind that comes from a person's soul.

"You know dawg gone well that you had no plans to buy an $80,000 fully loaded SUV! I have known you, Thomas Johnson, for a long time, and you're as cheap as the day is long. That's one of the reasons I got rid of your ass," she continued, seemingly delighted about this new line of conversation. Andrea loved to talk about three things: my cheapness, my perceived lack of taste in anything, especially cars, and her success as a black businesswoman.

"You didn't get rid of me. We kinda agreed that we would mutually part. Anyway, how come you driving a Ford and you work for GM? I always pegged you for a company girl through and through."

"You know this ain't my car. Mine had to be serviced so I took my husband's. The truth is I really like this truck and I drive it more than I drive my own. But you know I wouldn't actually pay for one because of my job," she said, slipping into that familiar, professional-sounding voice whenever she talked about her job.

"So what you are driving these days? An Escalade?" I asked.

"I have a blue Yukon."

"That's a stripped-down Escalade."

"No, it's not."

"Yes, it is."

"How you gonna tell me and I work for the company?"

She had a point, but I still thought I was right. But I had to let that one go.

"Well, you know I like to look at all my options when I buy a car because it needs to last a long time," I said, trying to project my best "I am an educated consumer" voice. I take my time, weigh all the opportunities, and read the consumer reports.

"Well, that's not what you used to do when we were married," she said, glancing at me with that devilish smile she flashed when she was in her element during our conversations.

"I did but I just never mentioned that part to you. That's why I never got stuck with a lemon," I responded, pleased with my quick ability to lie on demand. The truth is I never looked at anything but the sticker price and the miles when I bought a car and still didn't. I will always be a trust-my-gut shopper.

"Thomas, not to change the subject, but why do you think we really didn't work out?" Andrea asked.

And the first thing I thought was *Why do people say not to change the subject and then they change the subject?* She had tracked back to this conversation, and I was hoping that she would have forgotten, and I was sure I wouldn't have another near-death experience to get me off the hook.

I thought carefully for a moment and then said, "I believe we were too young and too much alike, because both of us were kinda headstrong." I had to admit I was pleased with my response to such a difficult question. If life had taught me anything, it taught me that when marriages failed, it could be for a whole host of confusing, complex, and often frustrating thoughts, feelings, and circumstances.

Andrea turned her head and looked at me briefly, long enough to make eye contact and smile. "Believe whatever you need to, to get you through the day. But that's not how I remember it."

After that response, I knew she was waiting for me to ask her about her version of what happened, but I didn't because I definitely didn't want to hear that sad song that blamed me for everything, and I knew it would frankly piss me off. I was in a decent mental place considering the circumstances right now on this trip, and we had managed to get through most of this part without too much relationship reflection drama.

I said, "Your version or mind, it's not important. I'm just glad we found a way to keep in touch." I just knew she would just dive into her "You were a crappy husband" dialogue, but she didn't.

"Agreed," she said.

Then the narrative shifted back to her other favorite topic, and she talked about how GM would be building more SUVs and crossover vehicles and fewer cars because that's where the market was headed.

As she talked, she seemed to become more energized and enthusiastic. Andrea was born and bred for business, and she was really, *really* good at it. When we were together, her starting salary was double mine. She even had a college internship that paid more money than my first gig with the city of Detroit. She worked long hours from day one and received promotions and raises almost annually. Her career was on the fast track, and both of us knew it. And that was part of the beginning of the end for us, but it would take five more years after we were married before we eventually crashed on the rocks of divorce.

On paper we should have been the perfect couple. We were both smart and athletic. But in reality, we started early moving in different directions shortly after we said the proverbial I-do's. She always said that I was intimidated by her success, but I never was. I just wanted us to start building a life together where I was the leader of the Johnson family and we worked together. The problem was that she also wanted to lead the Johnson ship and had the resources to back it up. And when two strong personalities collide, nothing good gets created, and the fallout is arguing and shouting and eventually detachment and resentment. And anyone with half a brain can write the rest of that story. After that, we lost touch for about a year.

Then I ran into her at a car show in downtown Detroit, and we just connected again. I was between girlfriends at the time, and she had married a doctor from Cincinnati. He saved lives and she put them in expensive SUVs. It was the perfect combination. I was truly happy for her. Andrea had a strong personality and always needed to be the smartest person in the room, and in most cases, she was. She had a heart of gold and would help anyone she thought was deserving. And that was one of the things I loved about her.

When I met her husband, I instantly understood the connection. He was an attractive man, soft spoken, and a bit mousey for my taste, and that's why I knew that they would stay together forever. There was no doubt who ran that ship, and it was without a doubt not him! They told me the story of how they met through one of her friends from school, blah, blah, blah, blah, and something about a cruise and flowers on a bed or something like that because I was half listening. He said something else about being inseparable and having an instant soulmate connection, his words being "instant soulmate connection." He was just too in touch with his feelings. He seemed so mousey I could have sworn that he asked her permission to go to the bathroom at the auto show. Well, I might not be remembering that right but that's just me.

Anyway, if there was such a thing as winning at life, Andrea was knocking that ball out of the proverbial park. Yet at the end of the day, my hope was that she was happy cause she had obviously figured out the rich part. This damn truck we were riding in cost more than my first house.

I also found myself wondering again how she convinced her husband to let her travel halfway across the country with her ex to go to a funeral. Lisa's death was so painfully one of those out-of-the-blue life experiences, and then the suggested road trip to the funeral. A part of me felt like I should have been offended because her husband should have been worried about letting his wife travel across the country with her good-looking ex-husband. What was up with that? I found the whole decision to be funny, not the ha-ha funny but the strange funny. Although I did notice that he had called at least twice as she attempted to talk in code by placing the phone setting to private. I also heard her mention that she was staying with a girlfriend while in Norfolk. She knew my sister lived there as well and that I would most likely stay with her and her family. I thought I heard her trying to explain where I was staying, but I wasn't completely sure because her code talk got very low during those moments.

"Not to change the subject, but don't you have access to a corporate jet for emergencies or something?" I asked, attempting to change the subject away from any kind of relationship talk. "We could have hopped into one of those jets and flown into Norfolk Saturday morning before the funeral. We all know the car companies have them because they used them to fly to Washington to beg for money."

"Funny man," she responded, but I noticed she didn't say no. So here we were on the last leg of a twelve-hour road trip from door to church and I hadn't driven a single mile and knew I wouldn't drive a single mile either. I'll bet her fragile ass husband told her to not let me drive his expensive SUV.

Then she said, "If you're serious about buying something new, you know I can get you really good discounts, right?"

"Well, we will see cause I have to check some things first," I said, knowing damn well I wasn't going to buy a new car and there were no "things" to check. And she knew it too but thought it was right for her to offer.

She continued, "Well just let me know when you are ready, and I'll hook you up." I found myself saying "OK, I might just do that." Lie! Lie! Lie! Lie!

The stories we tell others should never be the stories we tell ourselves when we really know who we are.

"It's time for another stop for food and a bathroom break," she said. "Besides, I just need a chance to stretch my legs and not be in a car."

"I agree. Let's see if we can find something good," I responded.

Food was always tricky for me when traveling long distances. Eating too much and I would find myself forced to become acquainted with strange restrooms with varying degrees of cleanliness and purposely looking for any gas station that advertised clean restrooms. But in spite of the bathroom challenge, I still liked road trips. They gave me time to be away from my everyday routines and wonder about things I normally wouldn't think about. And traveling by car was also a time to just ride quietly and enjoy the passing scenery. It was on some occasions my therapy, a way to think through situations without having to come up with a solution and without all the external feedback I get from others.

We finally stopped at Mickey D's after a failed attempt to get chicken sandwiches from that other place. When we pulled into the drive through at the chicken place, I knew we would be ass out of luck. First of all, there was no line, just one car in front of us, and this was just a week after those reports of people running each other over or something like that for that new chicken sandwich. Every time I thought about that story, I couldn't help but wonder what that woman would say when she arrived in prison. Other inmates discussing how they killed their spouses with rat position or death by shotgun. And this fiery lady will have to say she ran a man over for a chicken sandwich. Now that's got to be some ghetto black stuff for your ass—death by chicken or death for chicken. And I'll bet she didn't even get the sandwich cause when you run somebody over and the police show up, my guess is that you kinda stop thinking about food and start thinking if you will be able to prevent yourself from becoming somebody's honey boo-boo in the pokey. When we pulled up to the menu kiosk, we heard a male voice say, "Hold on." That's it. Not "May I help you?" or "I'll be with you in a minute." Just "Hold on." We held on for about ten minutes before I started yelling into the speaker, "Helllllooooooooo! Helllllooooooooo."

Finally, the voice came back and said, "What cha'll want? What cha'll want?"

Andrea looked at me and said, "I see where this is going."

Yeah, me too, cause there's a reason there's no line. And in spite of everything that was happening I ordered anyway, "Two chicken sandwiches and two sodas, one diet," I said, leaning toward Andrea to be closer to the speaker and almost yelling as I ordered.

"Diet pop?" Andrea said.

"Yeah," I responded, "trying to lose weight." She looked at me with the "Negro, please!" look. I stared back as if to say, "Yeah, what of it?" But Andrea is always Andrea, and she exploded in laughter.

"I guess my life just cracks you up, huh?"

"Yeah, it does sometimes," she said, "but you know me so don't go getting all sensitive, because if I remember correctly, sensitivity was never one of your strong points."

"Ha ha," I responded, knowing this freaking woman knew way too much about me and she always had that gift of making everything about what I wasn't. Some women never seem to get over stuff.

The voice said, "$11.15," then I guess the voice realized that he wasn't exactly Mr. Customer Service. He said, "It's only two of us here so it might take a minute." No "I'm sorry for the inconvenience" or "We are doing the best we can." I guess we needed to assume that, but "Just the two of us." So if a minute were the same time length as "Hold on," then we would waste another fifteen or twenty minutes waiting to get the sandwiches. So, we waited for another ten minutes and realized that the fast food was anything but fast.

"I guess I don't feel like chicken today," I said. "We should try something else." I was completely annoyed by this absolutely terrible customer service.

"Let's give it a few more minutes," she responded.

In my mind, I said, "That's why our crap didn't work out, always trying to be in control." She knew we didn't have a snowball's chance in hell of getting any food from that restaurant that was famous for their chicken sandwiches in the next—oh, let's say about an hour! So, after another ten more minutes had passed and no word from Mr. Customer Service, we slowly pulled out of the drive-thru, headed out of the exit, and drove down the street to a good, old, reliable, crank-out-the-fast-food Mickey D's.

We decided to eat in to give ourselves a break from the road, but there was very little small talk. We ate mostly in silence and watched the parade of people in and out of the busy restaurant.

After our brief break, we were once again back on the highway and headed toward Richmond, Virginia. We were getting close now and would be in the Norfolk area in less than two hours, depending on traffic.

Sometimes people surprise us and exceed our limited expectations and blow apart our inherent biases.

We were finally on the homestretch, and in spite of the somber reason for our travel, I was glad to be close to the end of the trip. The snow was falling pretty steadily now, but it wasn't enough to make me nervous about freeway travel. As much as I tried not to think about Lisa, the thoughts about her were jockeying in my head to dominate my attention. I tried to focus on the passing scenery as I had done so successfully earlier in our journey and slip into zen mode, but I just didn't have the discipline. Then I felt a slight swerve as the big SUV moved toward the edge of the road and back again. I heard what sounded like a loud thug or thump and the vehicle vibrated slightly. As I turned to look forward, Andrea said anxiously, "I think I ran over something. Did you see it?"

"I didn't. What was it?" I responded.

"Some kind of animal. I tried to miss it, but the left tire hit it," she said.

"No harm, no foul." And why did I say that? Even before the words got out of my mouth, I felt a slight vibration and the tire warning light started to flash red.

"Something is wrong with one of the tires," Andrea said as she slowed down as the vibration increased.

"Don't you have those run-flat tires?" I asked, knowing that wasn't the case since something had obviously damaged the tire to the degree that triggered the tire warning signal. This drive was turning into a ride from hell. Almost jacked by a strange white dude in the middle of the night, and now we were about to break down on the side of the highway.

We came to a stop at the very edge of the paved area on the side of the freeway. Any farther over and we would be in a soggy area that looked like the perfect spot to get stuck. It was now completely apparent the front left tire was losing air and going flat, and I couldn't figure out if the large SUV had a noticeable lean or if I was imagining it because I knew the tire was going flat. The Navigator finally came to a complete stop, and for a moment, we sat there on the side of the road, slightly on the soft shoulder but mostly on the concrete.

I looked at her and she looked back at me as if to say, "You need to do something." So, I climbed out to inspect the tire damage. While we were off the highway, I still felt like I could feel the breeze the big semitrucks made as they zoomed along Interstate 95. If there was a silver lining in this new situation, it was that we were fortunate enough to break down close to an exit ramp, and if we moved up a few hundred feet, we would be in a better place to change the tire or try to make it to a gas station.

I stood next to the front left area, staring at the flat tire as if I expected it to somehow miraculously reinflate and fix itself.

Andrea looked out the window. "How bad is it?" she asked.

"It's definitely flat."

"You know how to change a tire, don't you?"

"Yeah, I know how to change a tire, but you're really close to the road."

I watched the cars and trucks fly by us at speeds that easily exceeded seventy-five miles per hour. And in my mind, I could just imagine one distracted driver going eighty miles per hour and drifting over to the side of the road just enough to run me down like a dog in the street while I attempted to change the tire.

"You need to see if you can get to that exit up there, and that will give me more space," I found myself saying and pointing south.

"You don't think it will damage the truck, do you?" Andrea replied.

"Right now, I'm more concerned with me getting run over while changing the tire."

"Oh, you got enough room, and I can watch the traffic."

"Why don't you just drive slowly on down a little farther so I can have more space and worry less about being run over? Too many stories in the news about people getting run over while changing tires along the side of freeways. And frankly I have no desire to join that statistic," I responded, a little annoyed about even having the conversation when she should have just said OK.

She looked at me as if she wanted to say something else because it was clear to her that I had enough room and was risking damaging her husband's expensive SUV by driving on a flat tire. But before she could figure out what to say, I started walking toward the exit ramp in an attempt to end the conversation. It was cold and I really wanted to ride the few hundred feet, but I didn't want any more discussion about the situation, and I definitely was not going to try to change a tire that close to the highway. Truthfully, I wasn't even sure I could change that tire. I had tried to change one some years ago when I was traveling in the northern part of Michigan but couldn't get the damn lug nuts off.

At first the truck didn't move. She never turned off the engine when I got out, and now it was just sitting there. I didn't care and kept walking as if I knew she was driving slowly behind me. I could just imagine her sitting there, contemplating her ability to change the tire herself, and if she did, I was going to get right out of her way and let her. Then the truck started to slowly move forward, and I realized that I had won this round as she had decided that changing a tire on the side of the highway during the winter was not something she wanted to do and that if anyone was going to take that risk or get run over, it was going to be the man, not the woman.

After moving forward a few feet, the Navigator stopped, and the engine was shut off. When I turned to see why she had stopped, Andrea was frantically waving at me to return to the car.

I walked back quickly as the cold started to remind me of the folly of my decision not to get back into the SUV. When I got close enough, she yelled out the window. "I got some of that stuff that fixes flats!", she said triumphantly, pleased with herself that she wouldn't have to risk driving on a flat tire. And as I reached the passenger side of the front of the truck, I saw the lift gate rise at the back of the truck.

"It's where the spare tire is under the trunk," she said as I passed. It was now more likely that she was trying to remember if she still had the stuff and that was the reason for the pause and then her stop, but I didn't care, and since I didn't know for sure, I preferred my version of what happened. However, I was definitely relieved because that fix-a-flat stuff was much easier than jacking up the side of a big SUV and changing a tire, especially since I was now sure I would never be able to get the lug nuts off. And I wasn't sure if Andrea even knew where the wheel lock was and imagined that we would have to spend a lot of time just trying to find it.

Like many women who had men, Andrea used to believe when we were married that her job was to drive the car and occasionally put gas in it, and when I was present, she wouldn't even do that. Anyway, that had been my experience when we had been together. I started to insist that she still drive forward to the exit ramp but realized that that idea seemed kind of futile now as I could watch the traffic myself as I squirted the stuff in the tire. I pushed her small suitcase forward, slid my duffel bag to one side, and lifted the lower trunk panel to expose the spare tire and two cans of Fix-a-Flat. I could see her grinning face staring at me from the front of the truck. I'm sure Mr. Perfect Hubby made sure she had not one can but two cans just in case, always making sure his precious wife, my crazy ex, was looked after since he was not there to drive her and make sure she had everything she needed.

"If this works, let's get off at that exit anyway. I need another bathroom break," I said to the grinning face peaking around the driver's seat. "How far can you drive on this stuff?" I found myself asking, and I might as well have just thought that instead of saying it because I knew Andrea didn't have a clue.

"I don't know. Don't you? Aren't men supposed to know that kind of stuff?"

"Only men who drive cars on cheap, raggedy tires where they are constantly breaking down. I've only used this stuff one other time in my life."

"So can we make it the rest of the way without changing the tire?"

"I think so, but if we can find a gas station at that next exit that can change the tire quickly, we should," I said, trying to sound knowledgeable about such matters. "We are kinda pressed for time since we got such a late start."

We were actually doing pretty well on time in spite of our leaving late, but I couldn't pass on an opportunity to casually check her on being late. And I was waiting for some smart comment, but one never came. "Score one for me," I said to myself as I moved around the truck, going the long way around the passenger side to get to the front left tire. I promptly took the stem cap off and attached the nozzle of the can. I looked up at the traffic, intently watching the flow and making sure all vehicles stayed in their respective lanes and on the highway. I wasn't completely convinced this stuff would work on such a large vehicle but was pleased to see the tire rise as the foam filled the empty spaces left by escaping air.

Within a few minutes, we were at a Mobil gas station and talking to a mechanic who said that he could put the spare tire on or fix the flat if we had time to wait. We opted for the fixed tire since the SUV had that small spare only designed to go no more than one hundred miles. So we ended up sitting in a small mom and pop diner named Do Drop In, located next to the gas station and looking at what appeared to be homemade menus, two sided with pictures of house specials on the back and all the other menu offerings on the front.

I wasn't really that hungry but felt the need to eat something so I scanned the menu, looking for something that would allow me to travel the rest of this trip without a number two bathroom stop.

Andrea, on the other hand, was a true foodie. She loved eating different foods and going to different places and had no problem waiting for hours to get into restaurants that were popular or unique in some way. I frankly didn't care unless the food included some deviation of chocolate and absolutely hated waiting longer than fifteen minutes to eat. The place was pleasant enough with a 1950s feel to it, red bar stools at an extended counter, red and black two- and four-seat booths near the entrance, and movable tables near a bathroom entrance sign located close to the rear of the building. We were the only black folk there as the place was mostly empty and all white, which made me wonder about the quality of the food and also informed my selective food choices.

While we were waiting for one of the two waitresses to come to our table, Andrea leaned over to make sure I was the only person who heard her. "You think it's safe to eat in here?" she asked in a voice barely above a whisper.

"Why wouldn't it be?"

"I heard sometimes white folk spit in black people's food. You think this place is like that?" She knew I didn't have an answer but wanted me to say something reassuring so she would feel more comfortable eating in the place.

"I don't think so," I finally said. "This place seems friendly enough and the people didn't freak out and stare when we walked through the door so we should be good. If this were 1960, then I would have to wonder, and who told you white folk spit in people's food?"

"You know that's what they say about nasty white people from the south," she said.

"You and I are both from the south and 'they' haven't said that to me," I responded.

"You know you heard that too, and you thought about it every time you went in some random restaurant while traveling," she shot back, staring at me as if to say, "Knock it off because you know black folk wonder about that kind of stuff."

"Yeah, you're right. I have heard that, but I don't know if that was one of those things we believe about white people or that it actually happened to somebody. Besides, how would you know? I worked in a restaurant when I was in high school, and the truth is most people are better off not knowing everything that happens in a commercial kitchen."

"Like what?" she asked with a worried look on her face, waiting to hear some vile act that occurs that she now needed to know about.

"Nothing serious, but just remember that real people cook food in a kitchen. Anyway, our bodies can handle a little food chaos," I responded.

Andrea stared now even more intently, trying to weigh the value of my words with her decision to actually eat in this current restaurant. It was apparent that she wanted more information, but no more insight was coming from me. In truth, I was just killing time until the waitress arrived because I had no such qualms about restaurant food and flying spit.

Then a short waitress with a heavy southern accent approached the table with two glasses of water. She was pleasant, friendly, and very engaging, and that was the final greenlight for Andrea. She took full advantage of the unplanned break and ordered a full breakfast of eggs, wheat toast, grits, and sausage. Orange juice was her drink of choice when eating breakfast.

It was the exact same meal she ordered when we traveled anywhere longer than five hours. *Some things never change,* I thought. I, on the other hand, took the safe route and ordered some oatmeal with scrambled eggs and a coffee.

The service was fast, and the food was delicious. We ate quietly at first, and then when I thought that everything was good, that we would finish our food and head out, Andrea looked at me and asked the question I had successfully dodged so far and was hoping to avoid this entire trip.

"Thomas, why do you think we really didn't work? When I look at everything and who we were and how we met and what we were doing, we should have been amazing together," she said.

And there it was. She had dropped the bombshell again, and like so many times, I was caught completely off guard because of how quickly this topic had ended earlier. And I had to admit I was a little sedated and fatigued from eating and traveling, once again not in my best mental state for this conversation. This time she didn't wait for an initial response.

"I feel like we didn't try hard enough to save us. We should have tried counseling or something, but every time I think back on that phase of my life, I get frustrated. You were really the love of my life, Thomas," she continued.

And I now found myself scrambling to frame an acceptable response. But I did remember some of that time and I definitely remembered going to counseling, at least one session. And as soon as the counselor didn't agree with Andrea that everything was my fault, she lost interest and didn't want to go back. I had had years to think about why our marriage didn't work and I had some pretty strong opinions about what happened. But I knew she wouldn't like any of my version of why we crashed on the rocks of matrimony, and we still had way too much time left to be together on this trip. And this is exactly why I didn't want to drive on a road trip with my ex-wife! Her real question was "Why did you screw up our marriage, Thomas, by being a jackass?"

I scooped another mouthful of oatmeal and chewed slowly, stalling for time because I needed to get this first response right, especially since I had a tendency of saying the first unfiltered thought that popped into my head in any given situation. I had done well earlier but was concerned if I could keep it up or if the old tell-people-what-you-really-think Thomas would show up and blow the whole discussion up. I raised my hand as if to say I needed just another moment as I was chewing and didn't want to choke. The stalling act reminded me of those old church ladies who would throw up one hand with their index finger pointed upward when they needed to leave church service right in the middle of the sermon.

"Well, I think we were just too headstrong and too much alike to make it work," I finally said. My mental mind guy said, "That's right, Thomas. Keep it short, and don't elaborate too much, cause that's when you get in trouble."

"I don't think you tried hard enough. You just all of a sudden got frustrated and bailed. I was willing to fight for us," she responded with a little too much passion for a relationship that had ended years ago. And what she said was just flat out wrong!

I saw that one coming a mile away, and it was all my fault. Once again it was what I didn't do. I bailed. I didn't fight hard enough. I didn't like that she made more money than me, and I didn't need to tell her what to do with her money. In my version, our marriage had been heading for the rocks a year after we were married. Andrea had no clue how strong her personality was and how she needed to control everything in her life, including me.

"Was it another woman?" she asked before I could formulate my next best noncombative response.

"No. I can honestly say it wasn't another woman," I said. They always go to the "other woman" thing because some women just can't fathom, that they are not God's gift.

"Then what happened to us?" she asked, determined for me to provide an explanation for the demise of a relationship that ended years ago and that I was perfectly happy leaving any and all conversations about it in the past as well. But I was like a rat cornered by a cat, and I knew she would not be happy until I provided some explanation that satisfied her.

"I think I just wasn't mature enough to deal with your success," I said with as much sincerity as I could muster. I had to be convincing, or she would think that I was just telling her what she wanted to hear, which in reality I was. She glared at me without responding, attempting to look into my soul to see if I was lying, to see if I was sincere. Since we can't see our own expressions without a mirror, I wasn't sure how well I was pulling this off, so I decided to continue since she had left the conversation door open.

"Our lives took off so fast when we first moved to Michigan and your career was going through the roof and mine was puttering along like an old used car. I didn't know how to deal with that, and you kind of got bossy and wanted to dictate everything in our house, and I had a problem with that too." I threw that last part in because it was true, and it made the rest more believable.

She still said nothing and just kept looking at me. Then her features softened, and she said, "So I took away your manhood because I made more money than you and had to make all the big decisions in our house."

See, this is why I hated these types of conversations! My mental mind guy was losing it. *How the hell did you get that out of what I just said?* I thought this but was smart enough not to say it. I wished I could see my facial expressions because that one didn't go down well at all.

After a moment, I said, "Well I wouldn't say all that." And then I had the momentary wisdom to stop talking because everything else that would have come out of my mouth would not have been good.

She sat across from me like I was some sad, little puppy dog, but obviously pleased with my explanation. What I wanted to say was that the real reason our marriage crashed was because she was a crazy control freak who didn't value anybody's opinion but her own, always thought she was the smartest person in the room, and expected everybody to get with her program or get the hell out of the way. That's what I wanted to say, but the rest of this trip would be even more miserable than the reason we were traveling. So I kept those thoughts to myself, and I sat there and took her pitying me for being a broken, weak, black man in her eyes. She saw me as weak, and I saw her as lost, and someone who really didn't know who she was, so she was always trying to be something else outside of herself.

"I'm sorry I made you feel that way. You of all people Thomas know that I can be pretty intense and sometimes hard to handle," she said.

I had to admit that I was surprised by what sounded like a half-hearted apology as my ex who wasn't prone to apologizing about anything, even when she was totally and completely dead wrong. I felt myself smiling and realized that my thoughts like hers about what happened to us so long ago didn't matter now. We were better friends than lovers, and if she needed to pity me and believe that my perceived male weakness ended us, then that was OK with me today. She extended her best olive branch, and I took it to finally close that chapter and keep the friendship.

What I had dreaded as a potential hot button of a topic that usually ended in arguing and cursing like it had so many times when we were married turned out to be a brief exchange and a quick reconciliation, wrapped in a little bit of lying. My words appeared to give Andrea a sense of closure, and I even surprised myself by how angry I didn't get and then I knew that I had emotionally let that relationship go a long time ago and had embraced our friendship.

After we finished eating, Andrea grabbed the bill as soon as it hit the table and left the waitress a very generous tip. We headed out of the restaurant and back to the gas station.

By the time we got back on the freeway, it was still snowing lightly, but the day felt better. We were in the last couple hours of the long drive, we made it through the night, this part of our journey together would be ending soon, and both of us would get a much-needed break. The anxiety started to rise in me again, and I wasn't sure if I was emotionally ready for the most difficult part of this journey, but for some reason I couldn't explain, I was glad that Andrea was there with me.

Closure is always difficult, especially at that moment that you realize that you will never be able to have a final conversation when you know you left too much unsaid.

The first part of the journey was well behind us now and the previous night that ended only hours ago seemed like something in the distant past. Even the accident with the strange man in the middle of the night seemed like it was something that happened a long time ago. The big SUV moved easily down I-95, and I knew we would be on Interstate 64 heading into the heart of the Tidewater area. In spite of the falling snow, we rode on easily.

Our conversations bounced around randomly as we talked about music from back in the day, dating in college, people we knew then, vacations we took together, other road trips and the places we visited, the funny times we had with friends, and the quirky members of each other's family. All the talk was a way for us to distract ourselves from the reality that we were going to the funeral of someone close to me and a person that Andrea shared memories of from our college days.

While we moved in the same circles in college, I never actually gave much thought to what each woman thought of the other. Andrea and I had an on-again, off-again relationship, and Lisa was always there with us, but she was always in a relationship. Henry was her man when she arrived, and at some point, unknown to us, he was replaced with Bill and there was no period through this process where Lisa wasn't in a relationship. But regardless of her status, she was always available when I needed her, mostly to provide me with some insight into women and to discuss the mostly brief encounters I had with several of them during my young adult years. The talks were always about some need I didn't meet or about my general indifference to things that were important to them. As I reflected, I realized that I loved the conversations with her and never really cared about the advice she provided. Those moments represented a time when we had our chances to be a real couple. We also talked about life and family and all the things close friends discuss, but we never talked about us and how we really felt about each other. And maybe there was never an "us" conversation to be had. In looking back, I found myself doubting the true nature of our relationship and wondering if my memories and thoughts were more of a projection of what I wanted than her desire to be anything more than friends. Unfortunately, as soon as the Lisa thoughts started, the strong feelings of sadness rose inside of me and I knew the tears would not be far behind, so I struggled to shift my thoughts back to the remember-when thoughts with Andrea.

Once we arrived in the Tidewater area, we went directly to Andrea's friend's house in Virginia Beach. The home was a three-story townhouse located near a small tot lot and a row of black mailboxes. From what I can remember, the subdivision of townhouses was no more than twenty minutes from the beach and the Atlantic Ocean.

Her friend Casandra enthusiastically invited us into her home, and we were glad to finally be off the road. I didn't remember her from our days in school but from the conversations they had she was definitely around. Casandra was a small woman with a lot of energy. She was a hugger and a cheek kisser and radiated a positive welcoming vibe. During our brief visit, she kept offering food as I repeatedly and politely declined. She would lose herself in a conversation with Andrea and ten minutes later offer me something to eat again. We were there about an hour before we decided that it was time to change and head to the church, wanting to make sure we arrived early and before the inevitable congestion that always seemed to occur at well-attended funerals.

We finally made it to the St. Paul Missionary Baptist Church in Norfolk, our ultimate destination and the reason for our trip. We successfully arrived early as we got there in about thirty minutes before the funeral was supposed to start. This was a black funeral, so we were really about an hour early. Andrea maneuvered the car into a parking space directly across from the church entrance but near the back of the parking lot, farthest from the church entrance. She backed into the parking space to improve our chances of a speedy exit. We were a good walk from the front door, but I understood and supported what she was doing. The funeral limousines had not arrived, and the family would take up most of the spaces closest to the main entrance. There was already a young man in a black suit watching the orange cones blocking off many of the spaces closest to the church. Anyone near that part of the parking lot would have a hell of a time leaving when all the guests arrived. I wanted to leave as soon as it ended, not wanting to shake hands or explain who I was to the attendees and families that didn't know me. I wasn't sure about Andrea since we didn't attend any funerals together when we were married, but I knew me, and I knew that I had to get out and leave as quickly as possible. I didn't handle grief well and, in most instances, preferred to be alone. Group grief was even harder to tolerate, and I always struggled tremendously.

"So do you want to go in now or do you want to just wait a few minutes since we are early?" she asked once we were parked, and the engine of the big SUV had been silenced.

"Let's just sit here for now because we have a little time," I responded.

The gravity of everything was starting to hit me at that very moment and the pain and anguish slowly creeped into my consciousness and created a wave of grief that hit me as the tears started to roll down my face. I realized I was wrong, and I really wasn't ready for the agony and anguish—and the sadness and the tears. I couldn't bring myself to look at Andrea and so I stared out to window in a vain effort to conceal my crying.

For the next few minutes I cried, trying desperately not to become totally unglued. Andrea reached over and gave me a half hug and I cried even more, and once again, I found myself glad that she was there. Her face touched mine, and I felt the wetness.

After what felt like an eternity, I looked out the passenger window just in time to see the funeral motorcade approaching the church, the distinctive black limousines leading the cars. They moved gracefully, maneuvering through the parking lot until they came to a stop directly in front of the church entrance. It was all so painfully depressing. A light snow started to fall again sometime between our parking and the arrival of the funeral procession.

Professional-looking men got out of the cars. They were all dressed in black

117

suits and black overcoats, the long coats that leave just enough room to allow the tie to be visible. White gloves opened the rear of the first car that carried the casket. Five men appeared out of what seemed like nowhere, removed the casket, and manually carried it into the church. They were followed by four women all dressed in black and carrying flower arrangements. These arrangements were huge and beautiful, and I wondered briefly which one Andrea sent. One arrangement was covered with red roses and was shaped like a heart, flowers in December, red roses sprinkled with white specks of snow. *What an odd spectacle,* I thought. The heart arrangement was so large that one of the women seemed to struggle to carry it into the church. She was met by one of the men in black. He took the arrangement from the women at the bottom of the stairs, and she seemed relieved as she moved solemnly up the stairs to the church's main entrance.

Feelings of sorrow and loss should
be allowed to flow through us,
and we should experience them
completely because that is the
only path to eventual healing.

Lisa's husband, Bill, and their only child, Carol, appeared and walked right behind the men carrying her mom. Bill walked next to Carol, his right arm around her waist for support and comfort. He was almost carrying her with one arm as she was slightly hunched over, crying profusely. I always thought that funerals were the absolute worst for young children. The experience would leave years of loss and trauma for Carol that would result in countess sessions with a child therapist specializing in addressing issues of loss and abandonment.

Then other relatives started to approach and follow as well. These must have been Bill's family. I saw Lisa's father walking along with the others. He must have been in the second car along with members of Bill's family. Lisa's mother had died some time ago from cancer. It was a long and painful death, and her dad, Ted, never remarried. He was a tall, statuesque man, the kind who always looked good in whatever he wore, and during my brief encounters with him, I always was impressed by the easy and open way that he engaged and related with people. In confidence he once told me that he wasn't a big fan of Lisa's life choices but that he respected them. I interpreted that comment to mean that he didn't really care for Bill, who was significantly older than his daughter and frankly talked too damn much. I always wondered if Bill knew how Ted felt about him or maybe that was just one more example of me projecting my ideas on the situation. I always felt like Bill was tolerated more than he was appreciated.

"We should be going in soon," Andrea said as she too watched the pedestrian procession into the church. Lisa was a loved Christian and was very active in the church, and I knew it would be packed and there would be standing room only, and she wasn't even from Virginia. Even as a religious transplant, she had created a successful Christian family at Bill's family house of worship.

I didn't worry about our seating situation in this homegoing ceremony since I was on the program to say a few words of remembrance. I was coming face-to-face with another life challenge that I absolutely hated, as talking coherently through sorrow was not one of my personal strengths. I knew we would be seated near the immediate family so I could get to the podium at the appropriate time, and I knew it was time for me to pull myself together to now get through the next two to three hours. I wiped my eyes and blew my nose with a tissue I found in the door of the car.

"You're right," I said. "Just give me five more minutes and I will be ready to go," I said sadly, absolutely dreading the first step out of the truck.

St. Paul Missionary Baptist Church was a beautiful one-hundred-year-old church, and being inside felt familiar as I had spent my college years attending this church while I was a student at Norfolk State University. And like many of the connections from college, they were all created and provided to me by Lisa. She was a student at the university a year before I arrived. So her friends became my friends, and she was my personal orientation guide for most of my college life. Her connections made that college transition one of the easiest of my life. She was my personal guardian angel always nudging me to live and do what was right and correct. Many times, she was successful in this endeavor, but sometimes, she wasn't as I was determined to be only so correct. I mean, we were in college! This was the time to be somewhat of a screw-up as long as a degree was at the end of the four or five years of educational effort. Thinking about higher education reminded me of all the classes I took and all of the information I learned and never used. The whole experience felt more like an endurance and discipline test than a means of providing needed educational knowledge.

The church was recently remodeled. The vestibule area was larger and, now that I remember, existing because the old church didn't have one. In the old church, members and visitors entered through the double doors from the back of the sanctuary, and once they entered through the main entrance, they were standing in God's room, the main sanctuary. In the old church, the pulpit was directly at the end of the same aisle that you entered. Now there was an open, spacious vestibule area.

The sanctuary was a short walk down a spacious, open hallway and around a corner. The pews looked newer than the old ones I remember. They looked less worn, and the silver dedication plates glistened under the bright lights of the sacred room where believers came to worship.

As we entered the main auditorium of the church, I saw exactly what I expected, an early crowd, and I knew that Lisa's funeral would be a standing room only event. Latecomers would be ushered into the kitchen to watch the proceedings on a large projection screen. Several times when I was a student, I found myself in that kitchen because the services filled up fast at the eleven o'clock service, or at least that's what I remember. The most devout and religious Christians knew this fact and would arrive twenty minutes before the service began, and the rest of us would get ushered up into the kitchen. After two or three kitchen services, I got smart and started going to the eight o'clock service where the whole service happened in one hour, and then I was done for the rest of the day. Going to the eleven o'clock service meant that I might be late for a one o'clock kickoff during football season.

Bill, Carol, and his two sisters were seated in the first row, right in front of the casket. I didn't recognize the others next to them but did notice that an usher was standing at the end of the row looking in our direction. We walked slowly down the red-carpet aisle toward the front and were directed to two seats on the second row directly behind the family. I sat at the end and Andrea sat next to me. A lady with a huge blue hat with what appeared to me to be some kind of feather pinned to the front was seated next to Andrea. She looked pissed off because she had to move over and give up the end seat on the row. I don't know what the deal is with old ladies and that end seat, but she looked at us suspiciously and grudgingly moved because the usher was standing there basically telling her to slide over. *Some distant, wannabe, important relative,* I thought. *If she was that important, she would be in the first row with the rest of the close family.*

As we sat, I realized that the space was tighter than it originally looked. Every inch of the pew was filled with bodies adorned in their just-for-funeral clothes: top hats, multicolored and shiny suits with matching two-tone shoes and socks. Someone had one of those black walking canes with a brass handle that looked like the head of a dog. It was black folk at our finest, here to say goodbye at what was supposed to be a celebration, a religious homegoing, an earned reward for a lifetime of mostly righteous living, a reward that led to an eternal joy in a mansion with many rooms and a place in heaven with Jesus and God, but it never felt like a celebration. It never felt like something to feel good about, so in that respect, I guess we all fall short. These were the times when I questioned my own mortality and tried desperately to understand it all, and like everyone else who tried, I always came up empty of real understanding. And so, I sat silently as the whole world around me seemed to disappear and I lost myself in my own grief.

Time seemed to have stopped and I saw myself sitting in an empty church with just Lisa's casket. Bright, yellow light escaped from the edges of the coffin as it slowly began to open. The colors fluctuated between white and yellow as they seemed to flood the sanctuary. No physical form arose, just penetrating beautiful light. Then I heard female voice say, "It's OK, Thomas. Please don't cry for me." The voice repeated the phrase several times,

125

and then the casket closed, the light disappeared, and I was suddenly acutely aware that I was in church at Lisa's funeral, surrounded by people, and someone was talking, but I couldn't hear what they were saying. The daydream felt more real than some that I had in the past, but I knew it was just a momentary escape, and I still didn't care. I craved the dream more than my current, painful reality. My mind wandered away again, and I found myself standing in white light. No one else was around me, no form, no shapes, no people, no objects, nothing. "You know I always loved you, and I hope you know that. I loved you more than I think you really knew, or maybe you did know but were not sure how to respond. In spite of your hesitations, I know that—"

The thought was broken by another voice. "Thomas, you are up, and they are waiting for you to talk," Andrea whispered as I sat transfixed and lost in my dreamlike wonderings.

My mind was dragged back to the now, and I realized the pastor was staring and waving his hand and gesturing me to come to the podium. For a moment, lost in my thoughts and pain, I briefly forgot that I was on the program, and it was now my time to speak, to say some reassuring words to Lisa's family and to share some fond memory and talk about how she impacted my life. I had to talk about a person I had known for a large part of my life, a person who had been on the periphery of my early years growing up and moved directly into my inner circle in the last eight years. We shared some of our deepest thoughts and concerns, and I loved the beauty and balance that she added to my existence just by her presence and her willingness to always be openly honest and sincere in all of our interactions. She kept me grounded, and I loved her for that, although I never found the courage to tell her.

I felt myself rising and walking toward the podium as if on automatic pilot. I had no idea what I was going to say and hoped my ability to find the right words in such situations would not fail me. They say time passes differently for different people and the whole experience felt like a slow mental fog. My words were brief, and I simply said whatever came to mind in that moment. Besides, I knew that no one ever remembers those spoken words during such times, and I wished that more pastors would know that since some find the need to turn funerals into preach-a-thons. I talked about how she was the first face I saw when I arrived at college, how she was my conscience pushing me to be better than I would have been on my own, and how I loved and will forever miss her. In thinking back, I only agreed to make comments because I felt that's what Lisa would have wanted me to do.

As I left the podium, the pastor gave me an approving smile as he approached the dais to begin his eulogy.

The rest of the service was a blur and I just mentally checked out of it. I was proud of myself for maintaining my composure, but once I returned to my seat, I cried, along with the rest of Lisa's family, and I didn't hear a single word that was said after that. Thoughts of her flooded my mind and only intensified the magnitude of my suffering.

My mind drifted back to that dreadful day when I got the call from Bill, and that terrible time that would be the last time I ever saw her. The experience was one of those life moments that a person remembers forever because of its significance. I was tooling around in my apartment in Westland when I got a call from Bill. He said that Andrea had been in an accident and was in the hospital. It took him a long time to get these words out as he was trying to talk through the crying, whining, and whimpering sounds, an incredibly distressing sound for a man to make. I could feel his pain through the phone as he struggled desperately to share the unfortunate news. He was forced to stop on several occasions because of his failure to communicate through the crying and heart break.

A conversation that should have taken seconds lasted several minutes as he stopped several times to control his grief and regain his composure. I didn't ask for any details as he closed by telling me the name of the hospital where she was located, and my response was short and sweet. "I'm on my way," I said when I got the chance and thought he was finished. I think he wanted to stay on the line and share his grief, but I simply wasn't in the mood. He sounded terrible and I had no real words for comfort. I was never good at managing my own grief and preferred to be left alone when life forced me to deal with such pain, so I told him to take care as I hung up the phone.

I called several airlines for a flight out that same day and was absolutely annoyed by the ridiculous price I had to pay and how all of the prices were about the same, one of many reasons why I hated to fly and took that mode of transportation only when I had no viable alternative. It would take me months to pay that credit card bill off! But by five o'clock that evening, I was on a Delta flight to Norfolk to see just how bad the situation was, as I was praying and hoping that she would have a speedy recovery and that I would be able to see her when I arrived.

Acceptance of others without judgment
or criticism is one of the highest
forms of our evolved humanity.

The flight wasn't full, and I wound up next to a middle-aged, thin, woman who looked to be in her mid to late forties. She was dressed in one of those old lady dresses with big red, blue, and yellow flowers. She had a cute, round face that stood in stark contrast to her very think mannequin-like physique. She carried a large, brown purse along with an even larger black handbag.

"How are you doing today?" she said with a nervous smile as she took off her heavy overcoat to make herself more comfortable as she sat down, dumping her belongings into the seat between us.

"Fine," I responded as politely as I could as I watched her jam her big carry-on bags under the seat in front of her. I could tell as soon as she was seated that this church lady was a talker, and while I didn't mind the casual flying conversations that often occurred between complete strangers, I wasn't in the mood for one on this flight.

The pilot had just announced that we would be delayed as they de-iced the plane but assured us that we would arrive on time as they would make up the time once airborne. I always felt like they fudged those numbers anyway so they wouldn't be late. The church lady looked at me and smiled, and then she asked me if this was my first flight.

"No, but I don't particularly like the whole process of flying, and I really don't like the idea of being in a skinny tube thirty thousand feet from the ground," I said offhandedly and thinking I was being clever with my response.

Then the church lady looked at me with an expression that can only be described as utter terror, and I realized at that moment that this was probably her first plane trip. Seeing her distress, I tried to say something to put her mind at ease because I kept imagining her jumping up and running through the plane screaming when we were in midflight and having to be tackled to the floor and finally being restrained and taped to her seat. I didn't know if they taped panicked passengers to their seats, but the thought was interesting all the same.

"That's just me, but flying is safer than driving," I said. "It's not my favorite way to travel but it's really the best way to travel when you're in a hurry," I continued.

My words didn't help, and she looked even more shaken. I think she thought I was trying to hide some hidden truth about flying. At that moment, she reached under the seat in front of her and pulled out the big, oversized bag. She reached in, retrieved a blue monogrammed Bible from the bag, placed it on the empty seat between me and her, and quickly slipped that bag back under the seat. And I was not surprised at all that this lady had a monogrammed Bible, because even without it, she looked like a devout, certified, and bona fide church lady. The name embossed in gold letters on the lower right-hand corner read, "Wilma Jean." When I saw the name, I instantly thought that there was no way she could be from Detroit with a name like Wilma Jean. That name was country as hell, and I found myself wondering if she was visiting someone in Michigan and for some reason had to fly back to some place in Virginia because I couldn't imagine this woman flying to Detroit in the first place.

She lifted the Bible and placed it on the pull-down tray. With her left hand, she flipped through the book with the dexterity of a seasoned Christian. Whatever passage she was looking for, she found it within seconds and started to read it. I watched her lips move, but no sound came from her mouth. Whatever scripture she was reading had her undivided attention, and the rest of the world faded temporarily into the background. *Oh Lord, poor Wilma is going to freak out when this plane leaves the ground and climbs to its normal cruising altitude,* I thought, and I would be at the epicenter of the drama, experiencing it all as I sat next to her, only one seat removed. At that point, I slowly pulled down the window shade. The little man inside my head said this would be a wise thing to do as I knew from experience that panicked people can be dangerous as hell to themselves and to those closest to them.

I started to say something else, but since my words had sent the woman into her current crisis, I decided that I had done enough and resigned myself to the fact this flight would, one way or another, be one of the most interesting I was going to take. At that point, I sent up a little prayer of my own that we arrive safely and in one piece. A steward passed our seats and told Wilma to fold her tray back to its upright position as we were about to leave.

We sat for another five minutes or so, and out of curiosity I lifted the window shade slightly and the men who were there before were gone, which meant the deicing effort was over and that we would be taxing out to take off. And before the thought faded in my mind, the captain came on the intercom system and said we would be leaving shortly. Almost on cue and within minutes of the announcement, the big 737 Boeing was moving in that slow, steady movement they make as they taxi out to the runway and get ready for takeoff.

I guess the scripture wasn't completely working because Wilma looked worse than ever. Her facial expression changed from intense concentration back to sheer terror.

She put the Bible back into the seat between us when the plane started to move. Then she closed her eyes and gripped both armrests like a person bracing herself for a punch in the face. Her lips were still moving but faster now and I could hear some of the words as the fear slowly wore down discretion for poor Wilma. She was trying desperately to keep it together but was starting to fail miserably.

It was at that point that I pressed the call button to summon a stewardess. A young woman appeared and seemed annoyed as everyone was seated and strapped in for takeoff, even the host staff. When she got to our row, I pointed at Wilma without saying a word. Her eyes were closed tightly, and she didn't see me point or the stewardess standing there next to her seat.

"Ma'am are you OK?" the stewardess asked in that polite rehearsed voice that they use when they think that they are about to deal with a difficult passenger.

"Water. I really need some water to take my pills. Can you please bring me some water? I really need water for my pills," she said. She said this over and over as if the stewardess didn't hear her the first five times.

"I will get you some water, OK, but please try to stay calm cause everything is going to be all right," the stewardess responded.

Rick Tenmoo

"Water, water, water, water. I need some water!" Wilma kept repeating and she was getting louder and louder.

The stewardess looked down the aisle at someone, made a hand gesture, and pointed at her mouth. She seemed reluctant to leave the distressed passenger for fear that the woman would go into a full-scale, all-out panic attack, and we were still moving slowly out to get in queue for a takeoff because no one wanted another delay, and if the plane had to go back to the terminal for too long, then the deicing process would start all over again.

A steward appeared from the front of the plane carrying a bottle of water. By this time, the people across from us were staring intently at Wilma. I'll bet they thought she was about to have a heart attack or something. To me she looked like a volcano about to erupt, and I didn't want to get burned by the fallout. So I turned facing her with my back against the window. I figured if she went nuts, I would be able to keep her off me. The stewardess handed the water to Wilma, and she almost snatched it from her hand. Well, if I'm being honest, she didn't *almost.* She grabbed that water like a starving person grabbing a pack of those little peanuts they give out on planes. Wilma already had two white pills in her hand, and that made me wonder how they got there since I didn't see her go into her bag under the seat. She quickly put the pills in her mouth and chased them with the water. She didn't just sip, she gulped the entire bottle like a person who hadn't had water in weeks. The whole scene was pretty sad, and I felt sorry for my fellow traveler. By the time she got the pills in her, she looked like she was seconds away from hyperventilating. Both the man and woman airline staff stood by her seat, waiting to see if they would be forced to take additional measures. My guess is that the man was there in case she had to be restrained.

After several seconds, Wilma's frantic breathing eased. Thank goodness for that vacant seat between us.

"You OK now?" the stewardess asked again.

"I'm starting to feel much better. I'm sorry for the drama, but this is my first flight, and I got a little anxious, but I do feel much better now." She looked first at both the airline staff, then at the passengers across from us, and lastly, she looked my way as she wiped water from her eyes with the back of her trembling hand. If I had a tissue, I would have given it to her, but we were on a plane, about to take off, and normally everyone would have been seated, strapped down, and ready to fly the friendly skies.

Wilma said she was a little anxious. That was the understatement of the year! I was sitting literally inches away from

her, and there was nothing "little" about
that attack. She was two seconds from
losing her shit on this plane until she
took those pills that seemed to magically
appear from nowhere, or maybe I missed
her getting the pills when I looked out
the window, but I was glad the episode
appeared to be over. The male steward
walked back toward the front of the plane
and the female attendant patted Wilma on
the shoulder but remained in the aisle.
I figured she had decided to wait to make
sure old Wilma wouldn't freak out again.

The pilot came back on the intercom
and said that there were three planes in
front of us and that we would be airborne
shortly. As soon as I heard those words,
I looked over at Wilma, but she seemed
to still be OK. Whatever she had taken
was definitely working as Wilma not
only did not look anxious, but she also
seemed downright mellowed out, and the
transformation happened so quickly.

A few more minutes passed, and the big
plane made its final turn; the smooth, even
hum of the engines transformed into a full
roar as the plane started to move faster
down the runway. I found myself staring
at Wilma the whole time, and while I knew
it was rude to stare, I wasn't completely
convinced that old Wilma would be OK when
the plane left the ground, but she was
unperturbed and smiled and leaned back in
her seat. I found myself wondering once
again, *What the hell was in those pills?*

We moved easily through the sky and the plane was relatively quiet. People did what they do on planes: talk, read, watch movies and play games on iPads or screens in the back of the seats, listen to music, sleep, and go to the bathroom. The snack cart just finished our row, and I got some pretzels and coffee. I used to get water, but it made me instantly want to go to the bathroom.

The plane was in midflight and the fact that our flight time was a little less than two hours was reassuring. Wilma seemed to be doing better than ever. She was once again reading her Bible and was lost in the religious word. Then she put the Bible back in the seat between us and looked my way. I could sense that a conversation was coming as church lady Wilma looked inspired and filled with the Holy Spirit and needed to engage and share it with someone. And I was the lucky recipient of her joy.

"Do you know the Lord?" Wilma finally said, looking right in my face and I guess expecting me to blink for something.

"What?" I responded. I heard her but was stalling as I was deciding if I really wanted to engage. What I really wanted was for old Wilma to keep reading her Bible and leave me alone. I had started to think about Lisa again and was hoping that Bill had exaggerated the seriousness of her condition as I told myself that she would be OK and would be pleased to see me when

I arrived. I felt bad now that I didn't get more details, but I just couldn't stand the crocodile tears and the constant pausing from Bill during our conversation. Bill always seemed too dramatic and was prone to not letting the truth ruin a good story on several occasions when we had talked in the past, and I was hoping that this was one of those occasions.

But Wilma was persistent, and she asked again, "Do you know the Lord?"

"Yes." One word and no elaboration. *Now leave me alone!* I thought.

"Are you saved?" she continued. I wished she could see herself because her smile looked like the cat from *Alice in Wonderland.* It was creepy and I was sure it was because of her happy pills.

"I think so," I heard myself saying, trying to sound indifferent and uninterested, but it didn't work.

"You don't know if you are saved or not?" she persisted.

"Who really knows?" I said in response and turned toward the window, pretending to be looking at something in the sky. I even raised my hand and pointed at the sky as if I had just seen a UFO and continued to stare out the window in a vain effort to end the conversation, but nothing worked.

"I know I'm saved, baptized, and headed to heaven, praise the Lord. You should know this stuff if you were a studying Christian," she continued even as I looked away.

That last statement did it for me cause Wilma was determined to have this conversation and I really wasn't in the mood for her missionary work on me. And since I would never see Wilma again in life, I decided to be that wondering Christian if that would get me to some place where she would finally stop talking.

"What if there's no heaven? Have you ever wondered about that?" I said as I now turned to face my talkative plane mate.

"If you were really saved, you wouldn't be wondering if there was a heaven," she shot back, still smiling the Chester cat grin.

"I know, but I do fall short and struggle to understand some things," I said in my most humble voice. "Like how the kangaroos made it to the ark."

"What are you talking about?" she responded.

"The kangaroos. How did they make it to the ark? You know, Noah's ark and two of all the animals in the world. How did the kangaroos get from Australia to the Middle East where the ark was?"

Wilma looked both offended and surprised by the question, and it was obvious she hadn't thought about the poor kangaroos and did not have a prepared answer.

While she was contemplating the plight of the kangaroos, I decided to keep pressing. "I mean Australia is a long way to travel, and you must cross oceans. And what about the grizzly bears here in this country? Don't you wonder about how they made it? And what do you feed animals like tigers who eat other animals?"

As I asked question after question, Wilma quietly contemplated the implications and seemed to be in deep thought, and I liked it when she was thinking because it meant she wasn't talking. For a few minutes she seemed truly stumped, and the silence lasted longer than I had thought, and I was enjoying it.

Her facial expression changed from one of being perplexed to one of self-assurance. "You know man is a poor filter for God's word," she finally said, pleased with her response as if that was the definitive comment for such questions.

I just looked at her intently because to me her comment didn't even answer the question. So I asked, "What do you mean?" I liked the perplexed, confused look she originally had, and I was trying to take her back there for disturbing my comfort.

"The Bible was written a long time ago and translated many times. In that process some of meanings got lost in translation, misinterpreted, or confused."

Now I was impressed! Wilma didn't answer the question cause frankly no one can, but she did give a very informed response that focused on intent and not a literal interpretation, but she wasn't at all humble about it. And I realized that Wilma wasn't a humble, self-deprecating Christian but one of those cocky, "we have all the answers" types. She had that smug "and if you were a real Christian, you would have known that" look on her face. She looked at me like I was one of those non-Bible-reading Christians believing whatever the pastor said.

"That's why you need to know some of the history of the Bible, not just what's it in," Wilma said.

Oh, now she was just showing off! I had to admit I didn't know the contents of the Bible as well as Wilma probably did, but I did know quite a bit about the development of the book, and I was absolutely convinced that I knew that part better than her. But seeing she was up to the task more than I had anticipated, I realized now that she was ready and capable of talking about her faith for the rest of our flight, I decided to go in another direction in an effort to quickly end this conversation.

"Yeah, I guess you are right," I said, acquiescing, giving her the moral, religious victory she was looking for and hoping that would end the conversation, but Wilma's perceived religious superiority motivated her to continue. In me she saw a fellow Christian ignorant of the word and the history of the Bible and felt the need to take advantage of this teachable moment.

"That's why you have to go to Bible study, and you have to do your own study to seek a greater understanding. The Bible says, 'Seek and ye shall find.' Do you want to know what verse that's a part of and where it is in the Bible?"

Now she was really flossing! I was truly irritated at this point, like those times when Jehovah's Witnesses show up at your door and try to politely force literature on you. I didn't need this woman lecturing me on my faith, and I didn't appreciate that she saw me as some ignorant backwater believer. A few minutes ago, I was feeling sorry for her because she looked like she was two seconds from having a heart attack before we left, and now she was looking down on me from her religious high ground.

"Well," I responded as I paused for effect. "I do know the Lord and some of the scriptures from growing up in the church, but if I'm being honest, I believe that when you die that's it; no heaven or hell, no judgment, no mansion with many rooms, just dirt, maggots, or ashes," I said flatly.

That comment absolutely did the trick. Wilma's smug smile erupted in a look of complete shock and disgust. Her eyes bugged out and her mouth dropped open as she instinctively leaned back toward the aisle as if she were moving away from the devil!

"You ain't no Christian!" she said once she regained her composure. Then she picked up her Bible and gave me one last disapproving look and said something under her breath before she lost herself once again in the scriptures. I didn't fully catch what she had said but it sounded like "heathen."

No, she didn't just call me a heathen! I wonder what Jesus would think about those happy pills she took to calm her ass down before we took off. I knew I hadn't been completely honest, but I just wanted this random lady to leave me alone and it worked because that woman didn't utter another word to me for the rest of the flight, and that was fine with me.

It's funny how the mind works. I was remembering when I first heard about Lisa's accident and that church lady memory popped into my head as a part of the streaming relational consciousness. I couldn't help but wonder where that church lady was now and if she was still taking those happy pills. What I remembered most about the flight was that I honestly believed that Lisa was going to be fine, that Bill was just overly emotional, and that I would inspire her to get better when I arrived in Norfolk. That flight represented the last ray of hope that I carried for myself and the conversations we never had.

We learn so much about ourselves
when we stretch to do things out
of our normal comfort zone.

The next words I heard were "Praise the Lord!" And then the next thing I knew, an usher was standing in front of me urging me to join the processional leaving down the aisle toward the exit. As I looked up out of my stupor, the family was leaving. Lisa's casket was already gone from its place in front of the pulpit, and Bill and his family had departed from their front row seats. Emotionally I was checked out throughout the whole service, but I didn't care and was glad it was finally over.

I rose and headed toward the exit, following the other members of the family. Lisa's dad was ahead of me, and I could see his shoulders shaking as he slowly lost control, his strength and coolness fading quickly as it often did when strong men were stricken by sorrow.

I found myself hoping that he would be OK again at some point in his life. With people and grief, some learn to live with the pain until it becomes something else entirely, while others are broken forever and never find their way back to a life that matters. They never find the strength or power to put the life pieces back together again, especially when it involves the death of a child.

I felt Andrea's hand around my waist as she held me close in that comforting way women have when supporting a grieving man. *I hate funerals,* I thought. *I really, really hate funerals and never want one when my time comes.*

Right before I made it to the final exit that led outside, a small woman reached out and grabbed my hand. She looked very old but was well-dressed in a lavender dress with a matching hat and shoes, even matching gloves. She had a kind, grandmotherly face refined by years and years of living well. I politely stepped aside to let the others pass, and Andrea stayed right by my side. She looked as surprised as me. I had no clue who this sweet little old lady was. She motioned me to bend over slightly so she could tell me something that obviously was meant just for me. I obeyed.

"They say you were the one she should have married," she said, then she flashed me a bid broad smile as if she had just imparted some life-changing wisdom.

I didn't know what to say or how to respond to that comment. Failing to come up with anything else and wanting this awkward situation to end, I lightly squeezed her hand and said, "Thank you. I loved her too." And that was the best I could do, and it was the truth, but it felt so completely inadequate.

We all want to say the right thing at the right time, but real life doesn't make us that verbally poetic and we say the first thing that comes to mind. She seemed pleased and satisfied with my response and quietly walked away.

As we headed out of the church, I realized that she never told me her name, but for some reason that will never be known to me that little old lady wanted me to know what "they" said.

After two and a half hours of what was sheer suffering for me, we had finally made our way back to Andrea's SUV. The decision to park in the back of the lot didn't pay off as much as I had hoped because cars were literally everywhere. They were even parked on the grassy areas of the lot. Some of the bolder attendees actually parked directly in parking lanes and blocked properly parking cars in. Those people blocked in would have to wait until the illegally parked folk moved their cars. There were going to be several pissed-off folks in a few minutes if the cars were not moved in time. Our exit lane was clear, but the line leaving was long, and we would have to wait a few minutes until we could get out of the lot, but we were OK with that because we had no intention of being in the processional to the cemetery. We had made that decision on the drive from Detroit. This funeral was at the end of a very long, very emotionally and physically exhausting trip, and the thought of trying to line up with other cars in a long, snakelike convoy was not appealing in the slightest.

The thought of the funeral convoy reminded me of a funeral I saw in the city of Wayne back in Michigan. A procession of cars was trying to go through a red light on Michigan Avenue and Merriman Road. I was sitting at the light as it changed from red to green. I didn't move because I noticed the little funeral flags on the windows of cars, but everyone was not that observant. One car passed me in the adjacent lane and proceeded to go through the light. Well, one of the cars in the processional was running the light and not stopping so they could keep up. That car decided that it wouldn't yield. The next thing I heard was the screeching brakes, and then I saw the funeral car speed up to get through the light. Those two cars came within inches of hitting each other. That close call made me leery of such efforts, especially since no local police were involved to direct the traffic though the lights. And I remember thinking, *I wonder how many people die in car accidents going to a funeral or to a cemetery.* To me that would just be a ridiculous way to go. Once again thoughts by association and the little nerdy man in my mind driving my mental bus, but at least for the moment I wasn't crying.

Gravesite ceremonies only added to my dislike of all things related to death and final farewells. People crowd around a gravesite for a prayer and a final goodbye. If the grief of saying goodbye to someone you loved wasn't bad enough in the church, the graveyard site farewell was unequivocally heartbreaking!

"What did that old lady say to you in the church?" Andrea asked as soon as we were back in the Navigator with the engine running as the warmth erased the chill of the cold truck.

"She told me that Andrea always loved me like a brother," I responded.

That's right. I lied because I felt like those words were intended for me and it didn't seem right to share that information. Besides, I was still trying to process who she had talked to and where she got her information.

"Oh," she responded in a way that didn't sound like she was completely convinced that I had told her the truth, but I didn't care, and she didn't push the issue.

So we sat, first in a brief silence, enjoying the warmth of the SUV and watching the cars leave and the backup that was occurring because cars from all different locations in the lot were jockeying for a place in the processional. One big, blue SUV was driving over the curbs to secure a place in the line.

That's a damn shame, I found myself thinking. Finally, after another ten minutes or so, the traffic eased up. Andrea shifted the truck into drive, and we eased out of the church parking lot.

"When do you want to go to the cemetery?" she said.

"Before we go home. I have nothing else left today," I responded. I thought back to the funeral and how I had handled it all and decided that I did the best I could, even though I wasn't emotionally there for most of it. And then I wondered what Lisa would have thought of my behavior.

"I need to be away from this place," I heard myself saying as the church faded in our rearview mirror and we headed to my sister's, where I hoped to find some solace until we were on the road back to Detroit.

We were both out of gas emotionally and physically, and both of us needed time to recharge. As for me, I needed some serious alone time and I needed to be away from crowds, death, funerals, and sadness. I realized that I still needed some more time to process the pain and the loss. During the trip from Detroit I thought I was OK and had resigned myself to the reality that someone I loved and trusted was now gone forever out of my life, but being back in the church where we shared memories, seeing the casket, hearing the crying, and just experiencing everything was all too overwhelming, too painful, and I felt tired and broken again. So I prayed for myself to find the strength to better process my own grief.

If we are blessed to be surrounded
by people that love us, we should
never take that love and support
for granted because it is a blessing
that everyone doesn't have.

We pulled up in front of my sister's house, and the big SUV came to a smooth stop in front of the home. I looked over at Andrea.

"I'm glad we came here together." I finally said what I had thought on at least two separate occasions on this trip. Then I climbed out of the car and headed for the front door of my sister's house. "I'll call you when we get ready to leave," I continued as I walked away, not turning to face Andrea. In my haste to be away from everything, I forgot to get my travel bag.

"Oh wait!" Andrea said in response. She turned the car off and headed to the trunk. The tailgate was already opening. She grabbed my bag and followed me toward the house. My sister was expecting me and heard the Navigator pull up. Before I could ring the doorbell, the door was opening. When she looked at me, it was apparent that I had been crying. My sister, Trease, was stunned to see me in such pain, because I wasn't the crying type. For most of my life, I had always believed that a crying man was never an acceptable look unless it was for the loss of an immediate family member who was close to the person. But grief did not respect male definitions of manhood and how they should express sorrow. Trease knew that me and Andrea were longtime friends with lives that seemed to progress in parallel tracks and that our history exceeded decades. So once again as I stood on the porch of my sister's house, I found myself struggling to process emotions that I didn't know existed or refused to acknowledge when she was alive.

"Y'all made it finally," Trease said.

I tried to smile, but my facial muscles failed. I gave my sister a half-hearted hug and quietly walked past her into the house. Andrea walked up behind me. The two women smiled at each other. To Andrea, seeing Trease was like seeing an old friend. Her heart lifted as the two women embraced each other.

"Girl, I haven't seen you since you and my brother split up years ago," Trease said.

"It's been a minute," Andrea responded.

"How was the funeral?" Trease asked.

"Sad, like most funerals, but I'm glad it's over and I'm glad I was able to make it," Andrea replied politely.

"I see. They were really close, and Lisa was like family," Trease continued. "Well, I'm glad you were there to help him through this. Even though y'all didn't work, you know I always liked how you took care of him when y'all were together."

"Thank you, girl. I tried, but you know your brother can be more than a handful," Andrea replied, pleased with the unexpected compliment from my sister.

"You know I know. Come on in and rest a bit. You must be exhausted from that long trip from Detroit and having to go right to the funeral," Trease said, gesturing with her right arm for Andrea to come into the house and out of the cold.

"Thanks, Trease, but I have some friends waiting for me, and when I crash, I'll be down where I fall," Andrea said.

"I understand. That's a nice SUV," she said as she was now looking past Andrea and at the expensive, large truck parked in front of her house.

"Thank you, girl. It's my husband's car. Here's your brother's bag." Andrea dropped the blue sports bag just inside the door, gave my sister another hug, and then she turned and headed back to the Navigator. The engine roared to life, the big car backed slowly out of the parking space, and it disappeared down the street.

I sat quietly in my sister's living room chair, one of those big chairs with the matching ottoman. Normally it was my favorite spot to sit and watch football when I visited. Having known me all my life, she knew that when I was dealing with anything, the best thing to do was to leave me alone, especially since I had just arrived from a funeral.

"If you need anything, let me know and I'll check on you later," she said as she left the room. She patted me on the shoulder and headed upstairs to her third-floor bedroom.

I was tired and exhausted, and all the fatigue hit me as soon as I was comfortable in the big chair. I wanted to sleep, but sleep wouldn't come. In spite of my worn-out condition, my body had to unwind before it would allow me the relief of slumber. More memories of my college years started to occupy my thoughts and I let them flow, without reacting. I was too tired to do anything but watch the mental movie of that part of my life play inside of my head.

I was trying to get to my car and go to the choir to practice. My class had ended late, and I made the situation worse by standing around talking about nothing of any circumstance. I was talking to Chun Lee, a Chinese student who was explaining to me how to make rice in a rice cooker, and I found that to be the most fascinating thing since I was a horrible cook and had tried to make rice but it always turned out too soupy or too sticky. We started with a casual conversation about eating after the class since it was close to six in the evening, and somehow, we wound up talking about cooking rice. She would eventually give me her rice cooker before she went back home to China, but I was completely fascinated and wasted too much time on the subject.

Before I knew it, was six thirty and I needed to get to practice. Then I found myself running across campus like OJ Simpson in those old Avis Rental Car commercials; that was old OJ, the one who had an amazing football career and the one all the white folk loved. Who knew that situation would go so sideways?

Once I reached the parking garage, I had to go up to the third floor and find my car. Lower spaces were reserved for faculty and other people who could pay a hundred dollars a month not to have to climb stairs or ride slow-motion elevators to the higher floors. I unlocked my door and jumped in my 1972 Nova limited edition car. Well, it wasn't really a limited edition; it was just really old and missing stuff like air-conditioning and a functioning radio. The car heater never fully went off, even in the summer, and the side passenger door only opened from the inside, but it was mine and it had a big engine and would move effortlessly every time I hit the gas. I turned the key, and the powerful engine roared to life.

At that very moment, I saw a piece of paper on my windshield. *Damn,* I thought, *another one of those flyers selling stuff I can't afford or don't want in the first place.* I snatched it off the windshield and started to crumple it for trash, and then I realized it was stationery with writing that looked like a personal letter. I pressed it flat on my dashboard. It read, "Hey, my name is Andrea, and I noticed you the other day. Give me a call and we can talk." So someone noticed me and my car.

The note made me smile, and my head filled with all kinds of fantasies about how this woman looked, and it had to be a woman because based on my experiences guys just didn't leave those kinds of notes. While I never got a lot of those mysterious handwritten messages left on my window, the few I did get were all from women. "I hate you and I hope you die of a venereal disease" or "Your car is a piece of crap and don't call me anymore." That was the usual stuff. But somebody looked at my car and still thought I would be someone to get to know! This might be my lucky day.

I backed out of my designated parking space and headed to the church because I was still running late and was not in the mood to deal with the moody choir director who always had something to say to everyone who showed up late. I honestly thought he did that to shame the late people, but it never completely worked because someone was always late, but usually it wasn't me. That was my introduction to Andrea and the last thought I had before I fell asleep right there in my sister's big chair.

The next couple of days got better. Spending time with my sister and her husband was an effective therapy for my grief. My nephew, Daniel, was three years old, superinquisitive, and a wonderful distraction. I babysat for them, and we played hide-and-seek, peekaboo, and chase-the-baby. I never thought of myself as much of a kid person as some of my other nieces and nephews were rumored to say that I was the uncle who didn't like kids, but the time with Daniel helped me to increase my appreciation for how amazing that phase of life is.

I was grateful and was starting to find my way back to my mental self, and now after several days, the time had come for me to head back to Detroit and my life in Michigan. Andrea was on her way, and my bag was sitting next to the front door. We had planned one more event to say goodbye to Lisa, and I was feeling pretty good that I would hold myself together for this last act of letting go. My mind had started the transition of internalizing all those beautiful memories that would play over and over again in my mind for the rest of my life when I thought of her, when I remembered the way she smiled and laughed, when we all used to hang out together, or the way she got frustrated trying to play softball when she couldn't figure out how to hold a glove. Some of those memories still made me cry. Like most people, I knew there would be good and bad days in the coming months, but my time with my sister and her family helped me to feel a little better, a little emotionally lighter.

My sister and her family lived in a big, three-bedroom, three-floor southern home with a sprawling wooden porch. Fake flowers in hanging baskets adorned the ceiling, and the centerpiece of the front porch décor was a huge ceiling fan smartly placed over a swing on the side of the porch closest to the entrance steps. When the weather permitted, this was the place to be.

During this visit, old memories from past visits of being on the swing forced me on two separate occasions to venture out in the cold to sit there. I knew from living in Michigan that enough clothes would make even the worst winter conditions tolerable. And on both times, I managed to at least partially enjoy the sunrise and watch the world wake up before my eyes. These early mornings were a time when I would be alone, and they afforded me the chance to become comfortable again in my own skin. I embraced the cold of the morning on my exposed face, and I had forgotten how amazing the morning colors are during the dawn of the day. I tried to steady my thoughts and just experience the joy of existing and allow my senses to provide unfiltered information into my head. In moments when I was successful, I felt alive and connected to the whole world, and then the thoughts flowed back to Lisa and loss and sadness. I had hoped that the funeral would be my closure, my way of letting it all go, but I was still struggling.

I ventured out on the porch for the second time on the planned morning of our departure from Norfolk, and the weather was warmer than it had been. Most of the light snow had melted days ago, and the porch spot was almost cozy, except for the occasional wind reminding me that it was still winter in spite of the warmer weather. Nothing seemed to be moving, and there was that lingering peace from the fading of the night that hung on for those few precious moments before all the hustle and bustle of the world came to life. It was in those moments that I started to feel better, emotionally stronger, and less vulnerable.

For a few minutes out of the hour that I sat, I was able to just be—no thinking, no feeling, no processing or judging. I just sat and my mind was quiet. I leaned into my senses to connect with the world and felt that brief internal peace that reminds us of who we really are, who actually exists behind the incessant thoughts and reactions of our ever-thinking minds. I surrendered to the eternal peace that is the real source of our inner strength, and I tried to hold on to that moment as long as I could. It faded with the waking up of the day but the memory of being in that mental place sustained me long after the moment had passed. I was finally feeling like I was strong enough to live with my grief.

Feeling better, I went back inside the house and started to pack my one bag, hoping that at least for now that I was in a better place emotionally for the ride back to Michigan. I knew I would have good and bad days when I remembered Lisa, but for the first time since I got that call from Bill, I felt that I was getting to a place that I could sustain.

It's when we are most discouraged and tired that we should find the strength to keep going because we never know the blessing that is awaiting us just around the corner.

Later that morning, a horn blew, and I knew that was my cue to leave. I hugged my sister and her husband, kissed Daniel on the cheek as he struggled to get away from me, and I headed out toward the truck. My sister and her family watched at the door as I climbed into the big Navigator. We all waved goodbye to each other, and my journey back home started. But we had to make one more stop before we jumped on expressways heading toward Richmond, DC, and all points north and then west.

Andrea was wearing jeans and a heavy, thick sweatshirt, the perfect gear for a winter road trip. She looked more comfortable and more energized. She looked thoroughly rested, and I was glad to see that since she was driving all the way back home. I had offered to drive on our way over to Norfolk but was politely rebuffed, but I actually understood why: Mr. Weasel Husband. We had gotten lucky as no snow was forecasted in any of the states we would pass through as we headed back home, just chilly weather during the first part of the trip changing to damn cold weather in northern Ohio and Michigan.

"Hey, I got an idea. Why don't we drive to Norfolk State campus before we go to the cemetery? I haven't seen that campus in years, and I heard that it has changed a lot," she said enthusiastically.

While I had made many trips back to Norfolk, I hadn't been back to the campus in years. The last visit was a homecoming weekend more than fifteen years ago, shortly after the university built its own football stadium. Before then they used to play their games at Old Dominion University, a thirty-five-minute car ride from campus. I remember the games being crowded and the traffic downright horrible. My sister, my old college friend Wally, and I attended the homecoming festivities, which for us meant going to the annual homecoming parade and attending the game. The football team was never any good for all the years I attended that school and most of the spectators came to watch the band perform. That's a sad commentary for a football team when the main motivation for attendance was to watch the halftime show, but that's how it was for many of the historically black colleges. The schools had amazing bands that put on an amazing show that was fun to watch and hear. And the parade was downright hilarious. The band was made up of alumni and current members, and for the most part, the former students kept pace and played as well as they had back in the day. With the two groups together, the band was massive, loud, and entertaining. Then there were the dancing girls. Time or reason had not been so kind to this group as the former girls, now grown ass women, squeezed into tights made to fit twenty-year-old female students. For some of the alumni women, stuff was giggling and shaking all over the place! At times it was difficult to watch, like slowing down to watch a car crash when you know you should keep moving.

My thoughts filled me with nostalgia for a time in my life that was filled with fun, learning, friendships, and exploration.

And since I wasn't in a hurry to go to Lisa's gravesite, I found myself saying, "Yeah, that's a good idea."

"You still keep in touch with that guy you used to hang out with at school?" Andrea asked as we pulled out of the housing complex and headed toward downtown Norfolk.

"Wally? Is that who you are talking about?" I asked.

"Yeah, that guy. I remember the first time I saw you, and you were with him," Andrea said.

"I don't remember that," I replied, somewhat frustrated with my poor recollection abilities.

"Of course, you don't remember because you didn't know me then. I saw you out the cafeteria window. You and he walked over to a green, old, raggedy-looking car. Then you went and got a clothes hanger out of another car and then you all tried unlocking the door. It was funny to watch, and I had a ringside seat. Then that campus police car pulled up and you walked over and said something to him. I imagined you saying, 'We are idiots, Officer, and can't get into our old broken-down car cause we locked the keys in it, and can you help us cause we are so stupid?'"

"That's what you thought? Pretty funny. Ha ha. You once again had jokes even before I met you," I said, a bit surprised by this new information that I had never heard before and couldn't recall.

"Then the cop got a long, metal stick from his car and stuck it in the window, and in seconds he had the door open. And what was even funnier was that you took that bent-up clothes hanger back to what I assumed was your car and put it in the trunk like it was some kind of real tool!"

Remembering this made Andrea explode in laughter.

"You never know what you'll need when you have an older car that could be prone to break down," I said, thinking how funny I must have looked saving a bent, ten-cent clothes hanger.

"Really, Thomas, a clothes hanger that you couldn't use even to hang clothes on anymore. Sometimes you are just one strange man in how you process and see the world."

"Strange only to those who don't understand the person that is me," I said, smiling broadly.

"Thomas, don't nobody understand you completely, not even your own family. You're like one of those old souls, the kind that come along every ten or so years in a family, the kind that people can appreciate from a distance but will never really know."

"Who you calling old? I'll take the strange person's comment but not the old part," I said in jest.

"Sometimes … I remember wanting to meet you after I watched your comedy show with your friend Wally. That's when I decided to leave that note on your car."

"I remember being in a parking garage when I got that note."

"A parking garage? Thomas, you were parked in that lot next to the cafeteria and Wally was parked on the street. That's how I knew what your car looked like, and when I saw the southern tag, I felt like that was fate."

"You sure it wasn't a parking garage?" I asked.

"What student parking garages do you remember when we were there?"

"Damn, I could have sworn it was in a parking garage."

"I remember writing the note while I was in the cafeteria and then waiting until you left. You grabbed your book bag and headed off to class, and Wally drove off once he got in his car. That's when I left the note about wanting to meet you and left my number."

"I'll be double damned. Why did I think it was a parking garage?"

"Trust me, Thomas. It wasn't a parking garage. It was the lot facing that main street where you enter campus."

For a moment I was mentally lost as I tried to reconcile what Andrea was telling me and how I remembered the story, and the more I thought about it, the more I realized that she was right. Where in the hell did I get that parking lot memory? I read somewhere that as we age our memories change and we don't recollect events in ways they actually happened. I knew something related to a woman happened in a parking lot somewhere in my past. I think.

"And it was great that you called me the next day, and the funny thing is that our first unofficial date was when I met you at the same cafeteria where I first saw you."

"We only had one cafeteria."

"You messing up the memory, Thomas, with your dry facts," she said jokingly.

"It was cool getting that secret admirer note," I finally said as I clearly remembered that part of our stroll down memory lane.

"We had a lot of fun then. We were young, had almost no money, but those were some of the best years of my life," she said, remembering a time that could only fully be appreciated in retrospect.

"We really don't appreciate how amazing and carefree life can be when we're young, and then time passes, and youth fades, and it seems like only then do we start to connect the dots."

Andrea sighed, and I got it.

For the next few minutes, we lost ourselves in our own memories of youth. I watched the cars pass as I looked out the window and found myself wondering not about the years past but the next phase of my life, about what was next for me when I went back to my life in Michigan, back to the cold and the snow, back to my job and my daily routines. I knew I needed to do something different. I needed a change but was unsure what to change and to what end. Those thoughts only depressed me, and I decided that I would let it all unfold as I always had and deal with my life details as they arrived.

After what felt like a very short car ride, we turned off the freeway and onto the main road that would take us to the main campus entrance.

Andrea had handled the traffic with ease as she moved in and out of lanes to maintain her speed. The traffic was light this time of the day, several hours before the rush hour grinded the travel down to five or ten miles an hour for long stretches in the Hampton Roads metro area. Our goal was to be well on our way and out of the area and long gone before that happened.

As we pulled into the campus, we found a visitor parking lot near the south end, near the new football stadium. We passed the very entrance we had been discussing and the parking lot was still there, but access was now blocked by one of those multicolored toll gates connected to a guard booth.

The lot we finally pulled into had numbers and strategically placed pay stations, but we ignored them as we left the SUV. Most students were gone during Christmas break and the pedestrian traffic was very light. The campus looked almost completely deserted, except for a few wondering souls. Some I supposed were students who couldn't leave for a variety of reasons. The few others we saw appeared to be campus employees.

The sun was shining, and in spite of everything, I was in a pretty good mood and looking forward to being on campus and seeing all the changes. Universities were small cities unto themselves, and they grew and changed just like old neighborhoods going through gentrification. It was always interesting to me to see the differences, to see how the old pictures I had in my head matched up with what was now existing on the ground.

We walked west together, looking around like country folk in the city for the first time. The campus was very different from the time we were students. We saw some of the old familiar buildings, but we also saw two very large, modern buildings that seemed out of scale with the older, smaller ones. The main administration building anchored the western portion of the campus and was the tallest building during our time. The library sat at the midway point and was always one of my favorite places as a student. I would spend hours there reading, checking out books, looking up information on microfiche, and of course meeting girls. On many cold days, it was a haven, a place to go between classes, a place to write papers on word processors and then print them on dot matrix printers, equipment that was much too expensive for the average student to buy. The campus was connected by a spiderweb series of sidewalks and walkways and open green areas where students sat, played, and socialized when the weather and the season permitted.

I had to admit it did feel good to be back on campus, a place that still felt very comfortable, very familiar, a place with so many memories.

"Where do you want to go first?" Andrea said as we slowly walked west.

"No place in particular. I just want to walk around and take it all in," I said.

So we walked toward the library and shared stories of our own experiences for that place. Then we walked west again toward the administration building and shared stories about financial aid, scholarships, and graduation.

"You remember, Thomas, how they held up your scholarship because they didn't like your scholarship picture?" Andrea said as we walked.

"No, I hadn't remembered until you just brought it up. I don't remember telling you about that, but now I do. I had on my fly blue and white sweater, and they said it was too casual."

"You were pretty pissed off if I remember correctly."

"Yeah, I was. Back then I was wrapped way too tight, as I think about it now. A lot of things I thought were important, ideas that I wanted to draw lines in the sand about seem kind of stupid now."

"Age sometimes gives us perspective," she said in response.

"For some of us I agree. For others we never figure that out," I said.

Once we arrived at the admin building, we walked around and made a loop as we passed frat houses and several of the dormitories located on that part of the campus. Our stroll was slow and easy as we passed the occasional person heading or leaving one of the buildings.

"Did you like living in the dorms?" I asked as we approached one of the girls' dorms.

"I think I just tolerated it like everybody else," she responded. "What about you?"

"It wasn't that bad because I only had one roommate and his girlfriend wasn't even in the country, so it was pretty peaceful, but it was so much better when I moved off campus."

"Do you remember why we stopped seeing each other at the end of our freshman year?" she asked casually.

I knew she remembered why but she wanted to have this conversation just to see what I remembered. I had already blown the windshield note memory and felt that I needed to get this one halfway right or the ride back to Michigan would be an interesting one.

"Well as I remembered it, you stopped seeing me and I assumed you thought I wasn't committed enough," I finally said after some thought. "One minute you were there, and then the next, you were ghosting me, so I moved on," I continued.

Andrea gave me a you-got-it-all-wrong-again look right before she started to tell me what she remembered happening.

"I remember what happened like it was yesterday. You were living temporarily off campus cause something had happened to your room or to some rooms in your dorm and you all had to move for a few weeks. Our heat went out and I called for you to come pick me up." She paused for effect, and I was glad that we were walking, talking, and facing forward because I wasn't remembering any of this. "I wanted you to get up and come pick me up the first time I called you, no questions or conversations. And do you remember what you said?"

I didn't remember so I didn't respond, and I definitely didn't like where this conversation was going.

"You said to call you back in about thirty minutes and if the power is still off you would come pick me up. That's what you said."

"I definitely don't remember that," I finally responded, sounding guilty the whole time. "And that doesn't even sound like me," I continued.

"That sounds exactly like you cause that's exactly what you said."

"I must have been sick or something," I said in a desperate attempt to not appear so indifferent.

"Your ass wasn't sick. You just didn't want to come and pick me up."

"You know how old my car was, and it took forever to warm up, and sometimes it wouldn't crank up at all during the wintertime," I responded.

"So you don't remember but you do remember that it was during the winter," she said, catching me in my pathetic attempt to put lipstick on this pig of conversation.

But I still kept trying. "Bits and pieces, bits and pieces. I vaguely remember something happening." I continued in a desperate attempt to save face. We were now passing the dorms and heading back toward the midcampus quad area, near the library.

"Then, even before I gave you a chance to come back, you were strolling around campus with that chunky fat girl," she said, the frustration evident in her voice as she remembered those unpleasant events.

"Oh, now you just making up stuff cause I didn't date chunky or fat girls in college or any other time," I said as defiantly as I could.

"No, I'm not, Thomas. I was so disappointed in you! Then I told myself that you weren't worth the trouble and that's when I ghosted you," she continued.

"But you decided that I was worth the trouble, and we got back together that last year," I said in an effort to end this whole dark stroll down memory lane. I didn't need to say anything else because both of us knew what happened next.

I guess Andrea needed a reset because we walked on quietly at first and then went back to some of the more positive memories again, and this time many of these memories included Lisa, who was the organizer of group activities in college. We talked fondly about the bowling parties we had and how they started out as small events and morphed into twenty people trying to bowl on two lanes. I used to think that people just gravitated toward us, but it was mostly Lisa they gravitated to. People wanted to be around her, and she was always open and welcoming.

As we talked, I realized that I never had much alone time with Lisa. There was always someone else around. While I floated around college like many male students, the closest thing to a relationship was with Andrea, my first and last years of college and then our relationship and subsequent marriage after that.

"What?" Andrea asked.

"Oh nothing, just thinking about a time I had with Willy when he was chasing this young girl, I knew would break his heart," I responded, realizing I had inadvertently said something I thought I was just thinking.

"Did you ever tell me that story?" she said.

"Nah, too depressing, and I know Willy wouldn't want me sharing that one. But that was the one that killed that old, green car he used to drive," I said.

"Well did she break his heart?"

"No, not really now that I think about it."

Andrea smiled. "Did you try to reach him while you were at your sister's?"

"Nah. I'll see him on the next trip," I said.

Our visit was winding down, but I was not ready to go, not ready for our next stop before we left the state. I saw a bench near the library entrance, and we walked over and sat down. The walk energized me, and except for that one breakup conversation, everything went better than I expected. Sometimes it's good to remember who we were, and this was a good place to do it.

We sat for more than an hour, talking casually and fondly of the past, watching folk walk, by and just enjoying being completely present in a place where we changed from being wide-eyed graduating high schoolers to young adults as we made all the mistakes and missteps that young people make at that point in their lives.

As long as we have breath in our bodies, we have an opportunity for a new beginning, a new or different narrative that comes with its own unique and interesting life experiences.

"You ready to go?" Andrea finally said.

"I think so," I responded. "You know how to get to the cemetery?" I asked. Being back on campus put me in a good head space, and I had to admit to myself that I was nervous about our next stop and how I would cope.

"Yeah, I put it in the GPS. We should be there in about twenty minutes," she said with her usual confidence when she was planning something, even as minor as a short trip to a graveyard.

"I looked at the program last night and noticed the place is named Hazzard Hill Cemetery."

"Yeah, I noticed that as well. What a horrible name for a graveyard."

"After that, it's back on the road and heading home."

"You need me to drive?" I asked again, knowing the answer before I even asked the question.

"I may need you to as we get closer to Michigan," she responded.

I knew we would get close and then drive straight back to my apartment in Westland and I would still be riding shotgun, but

that was OK because I had offered and that
was all I could do.

After that we rode in silence. It wasn't
an awkward silence, but the kind of quiet
people developed after years of knowing
each other. By the end of the funeral,
I think both of us were curious about
our state of emotions and the graveyard
visit would be that barometer for how much
progress we had made since Saturday.

GPS was either slightly wrong about
the time or Andrea was just driving way
too slowly because the trip took around
forty minutes. The directions from the
funeral program brought us right near
the gravesite, although it wasn't hard to
find. The cemetery wasn't any more than
a few acres, and the fresh dirt had not
been leveled and a concrete slab had not
been placed over the grave. We spotted
the headstone was made of marble, and
it shined with that slick, reflective
smoothness that would allow it to stand
for years after Lisa and everyone else
buried there was forgotten. A print of red
roses was carved into the lower right-
hand corner of the stone. The red paint
was a beautiful touch, and I found myself
wondering how long it would last before it
too faded. The inscription read, "To my
loving wife whom we loved and cherished,
rest in eternal peace with god." If there
was a heaven, I knew that Lisa would be
there with her mother, and I imagined them

picking fresh flowers as they laughed and enjoyed each other's company.

We stepped out of the car and walked close to the headstone, being careful not to step on the portion of the grave where another marble slab would mark the location of the casket, resting peacefully six feet below. Lisa was buried next to a woman named Betty Williams who had died at age thirty-two. Her inscription simply read, "Rest in Peace." Her grave had a headstone but no burial slab. Thick, green grass grew in that space. The headstone had two vases on each end that allowed someone who cared about her to place fresh flowers in them, although it looked like no one had been to the site in some time. Dead flowers hung limply over the sides of the vases, their petals long since dead and fallen off. I wondered if the person who brought the last flowers was just too busy to visit or if they themselves had left this earth as well.

Andrea walked up next to me, and we stood there in silence, each of us saying goodbye in our own personal and private way.

"We should have brought a flower or something for the gravesite," Andrea finally said.

"That would have been nice," I responded.

Andrea reached out and grabbed my right hand. She bowed her head and began to pray. I squeezed her hand in response, closed my eyes, and bowed my head.

When the prayer ended, she hugged me tightly and headed back to the car. I don't know what she read in my manner, but she correctly surmised that I was not ready to leave, that I needed a little more time at the gravesite.

"I'll be in the car when you are ready," she said as she walked away. And so I stood there, transfixed. I didn't know exactly why I couldn't move, but I knew I was not ready to go, that I needed to be here by her side, at her last earthly resting place. I didn't have the energy to process our relationship anymore, but I felt the need to linger just a little longer.

I don't know how much time passed, but something inside me finally said that it was time to go, that it was time to move on. I kissed the middle two fingers on my left hand and gently touched the headstone. The tears started to flow softly, but I didn't feel the intense sorrow of a few days ago. I felt a peaceful sadness for all those things that wouldn't happen, for all the conversations and life experiences that would never occur, no life stories about bone closet experiences, no rocking chair evenings of endless chattering on cool winter nights. We would never have that chance to reflect on life together in old age, and we would never be thankful together for lives well lived. For that part of my life, that narrative had ended. Lisa was gone, and I would forever bear the pain of missing her for the rest of my life.

As I walked back to the SUV, my phone vibrated. I ignored it at first and told myself that I would check it later, but after three pulses and just before voice mail would have kicked in, I decided to answer it because I realized that it could be one of my kids. And for some reason, every time I went out of town, all hell seemed to break loose with my children, and it didn't matter that they were with their mom. Something always seemed to happen. So without noticing the number, I pulled the phone out of my coat jacket and slid the green button forward.

"Yeah?" I said as I approached the front of the car.

"Thomas," the voice said, "do you know who this is?"

I instantly froze! I couldn't move, and I couldn't think. For a brief moment, I thought my heart had stopped from shock. My mind struggled to process the voice, but it refused to accept its own truth. I started to shake, and I suddenly felt lightheaded. The phone started to slip out of my right hand, and I felt powerless to stop it. I tried desperately to get my mind to tell my hand to hold onto my phone, but nothing was working. My mental mind guy was on break, asleep, quit, or wherever his ass was, he wasn't helping me hold onto control of my own body. My legs felt like I was trying to walk in quicksand as they trembled, buckled, and then just quit all together. I felt myself falling.

I could see the concern on Andrea's face as she was watching this weird scenario play out and was now getting out of the truck and coming toward me. Andrea reached out with both arms as she failed in her attempt to catch me because she wasn't close enough. I thought I could save myself by grabbing the hood of the SUV but misjudged the distance completely as I fell. The last thing I remembered was hearing my name being called either through the phone or from Andrea. "Thomas! Thomas!" Then there was nothing but darkness.

In the darkness, my mind wandered back to the moment when I walked through the door of the hospital. I went straight from the airport to the hospital as I didn't want any distractions, everything else on hold until I could see her face, touch her hand, and confirm how she was doing. Her husband was prone to hyperbole, and I was praying that this was one of those times when his emotions took him deep into the land of exaggeration and benevolent misinformation.

As I exited the cab, I complained about the excessive costs of the ride from the airport and found some joy in the thought that services like Uber would change the personal shuttle business. I grabbed my one traveling bag that was more of an overnight bag packed in haste and stuffed with clothes and a few toiletries that would last about two days. Anything else would have to be purchased. I thought about the last time I saw someone die, and it was my aunt. She was one of my best examples of living in the moment, and when her time came, I was standing there next to the bed, and I watched as the light went out in her. The instant sense of loss was overwhelming, and the tears flowed almost immediately. I cried for the loss of one of my favorite people and for the pain of that loss on my family.

While I have never handled grief well, I was glad I was there when my aunt left this world, wasn't completely sure why but it just felt right, and I believed as I do now that I was where I was supposed to be. And as I walked through the electric double doors, I was praying quietly that I wasn't headed for a repeat of that kind of loss that is so up close and personal.

Lisa had been in my life since childhood. We were friends and then best friends when our lives brought us together at Norfolk State. I trusted her with my life, and she was one of the most decent people I have ever known. We were friends, but I never really knew what we were supposed to be. Other possibilities were never explored, and too seldom the space for those talks was few and very infrequent for a variety of reasons. Our lives unfolded as they should have, I suppose, as we moved in and out of each other's space and life experiences. I watched her walk away from a man who loved the very ground she walked upon to a man I once believed was bad for her soul, a man that didn't deserve her spirit.

Over the years, I on the other hand wandered through one relationship after another, not quite sure how to make them work and feeling as if the whole process was something I was completely incapable of sustaining with any woman for any extended amount of time. I didn't quite understand women and so gave up trying earlier in life. I did me and forced women to accept or move on, but I was afraid to explore these issues with Lisa, too afraid of losing what we had, and too afraid of her seeing the man I really was, too afraid that she would see my inability to make matters of the heart work. Since getting that call from Bill, the what-if questions racked my thoughts and my dreams as they fed my feelings of being lost, even to myself.

"May I help you?", the attendant at the customer service desk said when she saw me standing there in the middle of the lobby, overnight bag in one hand and lost in thought, looking around to figure out where I needed to go. Up until that very moment, I was operating on autopilot as I left the airport, and my sole goal was to get to the hospital as quickly as I could.

"Yes, you can," I responded. "I'm looking for a room for Lisa Morris. She came in yesterday, was involved in a car accident." She looked down at her iPad and scanned the names.

"Yesterday, yesterday, yesterday," she said to herself as she looked for the name. The attendant was a small, pale woman who reminded me of all the different variations of white people. There were white people and then there were really, *really* white people, and she was one of those really, *really* white persons. She wore a simple white dress with no sleeves and those thin spaghetti scraps. The dress exposed more whiteness that would have been hidden by a dress or blouse with sleeves. *That's a lot of whiteness,* I thought as she searched for Lisa's name. Her hair was in one of those 1960s bobs with bangs, but she looked no more than twenty-five years old.

"There it is. She came in early yesterday. She's in room 912." She said this before she looked up from her pad and was a little surprised when she finally looked up and I was still standing there. Before I could ask, her sharp mind figured it out and she pointed to the left.

"The elevators are down the hall, and around that first turn over there," she said.

"Thank you," I said as I walked away.

It's still nice to find helpful young people without attitude and suffering from a strong lack of motivation.

I rounded the corner just as she had recommended and squeezed my way onto an elevator as the door was closing. There was a woman staring at me intently as I executed my maneuver. Her eyes said, "Fool, can't you see that this elevator is at capacity, and you need to wait for the next one?" But I didn't care as I was too determined to get to Lisa's room as soon as humanly possible, and if that meant making some people a little uncomfortable and annoying the hell out of a middle-aged, angry, black woman for a few seconds, then so be it. *People are much more accommodating in other parts of the world,* I thought. I didn't know that for a fact, but like many of my untested beliefs, I decided that's what I would tell myself on this uncomfortable elevator trip.

I turned sideways so I wouldn't find myself staring in this woman's face, but I could still see her in my periphery vision, and she was still giving me the evil eye.

The elevator stopped at the fifth floor first, and most of the occupants exited. And as soon as space was created, the evil eye woman moved to the left as far as possible from me and looked in every direction but mine. At that point, there were only three of us left.

By the time I reached the ninth floor, I was all alone, and all of those travel and observation distractions disappeared. A sign on the wall told me that room 912 was a right turn and, based on the numbers, was a brief walk down the hall. As I walked, I refused to allow myself to think and just focused on the sounds, smells, and movement in the hall. Men and women in white and green uniforms moved through the corridors to conduct their hospital business, and it was difficult to tell who doctors were. I heard a baby crying in one of the rooms, and an orderly passed me carrying a tray of food that looked anything but appetizing.

Finally, I reached the room, and surprisingly the door was open.

Lisa's bed was near the wall and was the only bed in the room. There were tubes in her arm and a machine that appeared to be assisting her with her breathing. At that very moment, I realized that I was totally unprepared for what I saw. It had been almost a year since I actually laid eyes on her, even though we had talked only a few months before, and it was a tough conversation. She told me how unhappy she was and that she wanted out of her marriage but didn't want to leave the kids. She was also worried about trying to make it on her income as a single mom. My advice was short and to the point: leave him and get out. But in the end, she said she couldn't leave and needed to stay, at least for the next few years.

"Then come visit me and get away for a few days," I found myself saying at that time, "if for no other reason but to rest and be away from the whole situation." She said she would think about it because she had some things on her mind that we needed to talk about. And that was the absolute worst way to end a conversation when circumstances seem to snatch such an opportunity away and when we live like we have all the time in the world to deal with life's challenges.

Seeing her in the bed broke something in me, and a rush of grief filled my every being. She was much smaller than the last time I had seen her, and I didn't know whether that was from the injury or prior to. Life looked to have already left her. I slowly walked toward her bed, and I sat in a chair on the left side, closest to the door. There was a second chair on the right closest to the window. A jacket was hanging over the back, and I assumed that it was Bill's. He must have stepped out. A diet pop, half-eaten Subway sandwich, and two chocolate chip cookies were sitting in the windowsill.

I touched her hand and then placed it between both of mine and found myself hoping and praying that something would happen as she acknowledged my touch somehow, but there was nothing, just the soft feel of her skin against my own.

The tears flowed slowly down my face as I started to cry. The machine she was connected to said she was still alive, yet all hope was starting to fade in me, and I realized that Bill had not exaggerated the seriousness of the situation and that my thoughts of hope on the airplane had been misguided. As I looked at her in that hospital bed, I tried to control my grief, and the more I tried, the more tears flowed until I finally gave into my sorrow and cried loudly and uncontrollably. Seeing her in this condition broke something inside of me and released a wave of emotion I didn't know I even had. I softly kissed her hand. "I am sorry," I said to her listless body. "I hope by the grace of God that you can feel or hear me in that deep place that people go before they leave this world and go to the place beyond."

When Bill walked back into the room, my head was on Lisa's side, and I was still holding her hand. I looked up and saw him standing there, even more lost in sorrow than me. He looked like he had been crying for days. He was still wearing pajamas, and it was well into the afternoon. They were blue with thin white stripes. Our grief and pain created the only real moment of connection I ever felt for the man. And quite frankly, I knew he didn't deserve her time, her energy, or her love. But at the end of the day, she had selected him over her dedicated college sweetheart from Savannah State and perhaps even over me.

He said nothing and just walked back to his seat and fell into it. He looked exhausted and worn down, but of all the things I didn't like about the man, I knew he still loved her because Lisa talked about how he cried when they fought and she talked of leaving and he always begged her to stay, and it was that shameless crawling on the floor kind of begging, that awkward on your knees, hands together as if in prayer, tears and snot covering your face begging no one outside the house should ever see or hear about.

What he didn't know was that she had stopped loving him a while ago. She stopped being impressed or enamored with his good looks, his charm, and what passed for wit in his creative interpretations of life. I never commented when she talked, but I could almost feel something that felt like hatred and disgust in her voice when we had talked on those occasions. Little did I know that those would be some of the last discussions we would ever have. I didn't think that Bill knew how she really felt, or maybe he did but didn't care. Who knows what really goes on inside of people's homes with closed doors and locked rooms? Now he was sitting across from me on the other side of her bed, utterly and completely broken. I couldn't help but wonder what was going through his head right now.

"You need to go home and get some rest," I finally said. "I can sit with her until you return." I also found myself wondering where their daughter was right now because she was not with him. "If anything changes, you will be the first person I call. That way you can change clothes, get something decent to eat, and check on your daughter to see how she is doing with all of this."

He looked over at me, eyes puffy and red with deep bags protruding under his eye sockets. Bill looked like he had aged ten years since I last saw him, and in that moment, I felt only pity for a man I normally disliked.

At first, he didn't say anything. He just stared at me. He looked like he wanted to say something as he struggled to focus. He looked at Lisa and then around the room and then he stared out the window and didn't seem to know what to do with his hands—on the bed, off the bed, in his lap, behind his head. Then he would look at me and then look away, open his mouth to speak, and then he would close it and grimace. And each time he did this, right before he found his voice, the tears started flowing again and he simply dropped his head and cried into the side of the bed.

I knew I should say something or do something to support him during this suffering time but wasn't quite sure what to do. As I said earlier, dealing with grief wasn't one of my best qualities, and I was even worse at being empathetic and supportive of others. So I just sat there and said nothing and watched him cry.

After several minutes, he found his strength again and stood up. He wiped his face with his pajama sleeve and scanned the room as if looking for something. Then he became completely still and stared out the hospital window again. He stayed transfixed for about ten minutes, appearing to be lost in thought. Then he turned and looked at me again.

"I'm glad you're here," he said as he grabbed his jacket off the back of the chair and headed toward the door. When he got there, I thought he was gone, but then he did a small pirouette and walked quickly back over to the bed and was standing right in front of my chair. He looked at me one final time, then he bent over and kissed Lisa's forehead and finally left the room, closing the door.

At that moment, I felt truly sorry for Bill because he looked absolutely lost without Lisa, and then I felt sorry for Carol, their daughter, because she had lost both of her parents in that car accident. This poor man was in no shape to help anyone, let alone a ten-year-old child who could never fathom a world without a mom and a dad. But right now, that was all more than I could reasonably think about because I was struggling with my own sorrow and misery and missing Lisa more than I ever imagined. But I was glad that I was alone with her again, and this was what I needed. So I sat quietly, forcing my mind to slow down the endless mental picture parade, and I tried to allow myself to just be in that very moment.

I started my meditative breathing, and it calmed me. The only sound in the room was the hissing of the machine that kept her alive. I cried softly, almost ashamed of my tears and my inability to control them. The fatigue and the emotional drain of the day was catching up with me, and as the hour got later in the evening, my sorrow faded into drowsiness and then into an uneasy sleep.

She was lying in the swing with one leg touching the floor to push herself so the swing would carry her into the air and back again. I was standing on her porch, waiting for my best friend to join me, but he needed a bathroom stop before we left and was inside her house. She looked so beautiful, so free, and so young and full of life. "What are you looking at, Thomas?" she said, although she knew exactly what I was looking at.

"You," I said.

And then she started laughing. I wanted to look away but couldn't. Then she quickly sat up in the swing and stopped it with both feet planted firmly on the porch floor. "Come sit with me," she said.

"I can't," I responded.

"But you know you want to."

I said nothing. I just looked and her, and she was right about everything she had just said but it didn't matter. My best friend popped out of the house with an expression on his face that could only be described as relief. He walked over to Lisa and kissed her on the cheek, whispered something into her ear that made her blush, and then he slipped past me down the stairs and into the yard.

I turned when he turned, and we were both on our bikes and back out onto State Street within seconds. I saw her walking toward the stairs of the front porch as we moved away, and I so wanted to look back one more time and steal one more enchanted look, but I couldn't find the nerve. And so, I could only imagine how amazing she looked while standing there on her front porch in that blue and white sun dress, looking young, beautiful, and enchanting on that hot and humid summer day in Georgia. I didn't look but told myself she was smiling broadly in that whimsical way young girls do when they know they are young, gorgeous, fit, and desired by all the young boys in the neighborhood and beyond— and even some creepy old men who should know better.

We rode off, completely lost in our youth, and then the dream abruptly ended.

The closing of the hospital room door woke me from my dream and returned me back to my place in a hospital room, back to my misery and sadness. I looked up and saw a young woman who looked to be in her mid the late twenties. She walked quickly over to the bed and started adjusting hospital equipment and checking readings and injection points of needles. Once her task was complete, she looked toward me and said, "hello."

"Hi," I responded.

She kept looking at me as if I needed to say more or explain who I was in relationship to her patient. I said nothing and just stared back at her and that was easy to do because she was easy on the eyes. Once she realized that no new information was forthcoming, she took the initiative and asked dryly, "Who are you? I met Lisa's husband and that's not you." She tried to smile when she realized that her words were probably not the most empathetic during such a sensitive time.

"A close friend," I said.

"Are you local, or did you come from out of town?" she continued.

I assumed this was her way of making small talk or making sure I wasn't some random person she would need to be concerned about, so I decided to play along because she was cute.

"I came in from Detroit earlier today. Lisa and I grew up together back in Georgia."

It was now obvious that she had finished her duties in the room and now needed to verify to her own satisfaction who this new visitor was that she wasn't familiar with.

"My name is Thomas Johnson," I said to make sure she had a name, and maybe that would end her inquiry.

She stared at me inquisitively, trying to decide if I was telling the truth. After a few moments of contemplation, she appeared to be satisfied as the hard lines on her face softened.

"How bad is she?" I found myself asking.

"I'm sorry but I can only share that type of information with immediate family members, so unfortunately you will need to ask them. But I can tell you it's very serious," she said in her professional-sounding nurse voice.

Thank you, Captain Obvious, I thought. *Lisa's in a hospital with tubes and needles all over her body and this young nurse tells me it's serious.*

Seeing the frustration and disappointment in my face, she decided to share a little more information. "You know if her husband had conducted CPR on her after the accident and before the paramedics arrived, she would be in a lot better place," she said. Then realizing that what she had just said may have been inappropriate, she lost all desire for further conversation. She quickly headed for the door and said that she would return in an hour to conduct another check as she left the room and closed the door behind her.

I didn't quite know how to process her last remarks. I don't know what Bill said when they brought Lisa in, but I sensed that that nurse was around and got the impression that he was kind of negligent or less than helpful in the situation. I somewhat knew Bill and couldn't imagine him as negligent—incompetent probably, but not negligent. And it was at that very moment that I realized that I didn't even know what had happened. I didn't get anything from Bill when he called because of the crying and whimpering. It took all my patience to get the name of the hospital and at the time that was all I needed. My mind was singularly focused on one thing: getting to where she was as fast as I could. Now I found myself here by her side, right next to her motionless body with the only movement consisting of the slight rising and falling of her chest to indicate that she was still breathing. But in the end, I knew that knowing the entire story would not ease my pain. Because whatever happened put me here with a nurse that said her situation was "very serious."

I had heard such words before when my aunt died some years ago, and that realization started the tears flowing again. They flowed slowly, easily down my face, and I couldn't help but to feel a heartbreaking amount of guilt. My mind kept telling me that if I had acted differently, if I had tried to decipher our unspoken emotional code, that she still would be alive and that she would be with me and not dying in this hospital with a blubbering, idiot husband that she didn't deserve.

I cried so much that day I could taste the salt on my tongue as I sat quietly again in my grief and the hours passed slowly as the evening faded into night and the sounds of people moving and talking could occasionally be heard from the hallway outside of the room. A nagging feeling again kept telling me that she was leaving this place as I sat, that she was preparing for that next place where souls go when people die, that I was losing her forever.

As the night came, the sounds and noises in the hall gradually subsided, fewer sounds of squeaky wheels on beds being pushed back and forth down the hall, fewer voices engaged in casual conversations. The change reminded me of how normal dying is for hospitals, and that's one of the main reasons I disliked being in these transitional centers for the sick and feeble.

Then around ten thirty that night, the door opened, and Bill walked in. He was wearing blue jeans and a white turtleneck sweater and was carrying that same jacket I saw earlier in his right hand. He was still alone, and since I arrived, I hadn't seen much of his family. I knew he had two older sisters and I think both were still living but I wasn't sure. I never had much interest in the structure of

Bill's family. He now looked rested and somewhat better than he looked earlier, but the pain and anguish could still be seen in his slow, strained movements and the haggard facial expressions. In his other hand he was carrying two bags from McDonald's. As he approached the bed, he handed me one.

"I didn't know if you had something to eat so I picked you up something," he said.

"Thanks," I responded. While I didn't like fast food anymore since I started having health problems related almost exclusively to diet, I did appreciate the thoughtfulness.

Then he went back to his previous seat by the window, and once again we were both sitting there with Lisa, each of us dealing with our own misery for very different reasons. And again, I found myself wanting to say something that was comforting and supportive and still not knowing quite what to say.

I didn't know if Bill knew how much I didn't care for him as a person, and he probably felt the same way about me, but he never showed it in his words or actions. I would get the occasional stares during my brief visits when opportunity took me through Virginia and I stopped by their house, but all in all, I felt that he just accepted my relationship with Lisa as an old family friend. Besides, I'm quite sure it helped that I lived in another state and saw them very infrequently.

Bill looked lovingly at his wife as he reached out and softly placed his hand on hers. Then he leaned over and put his face into the side of bed, burying it in the covers and the side of her body near her waist.

And it was at that moment that I knew I needed to leave. Despite what I thought about Bill, Lisa was his wife and he deserved to grieve her situation in private.

"Well, I'm going to head over to my sister's house," I found myself saying as I got up out of the chair and walked toward the door. "Thanks for the food, and I'll be back in the morning."

As I reached the door, I turned to see if Bill wanted to say anything before I left the hospital for the night, but he said nothing, his face still buried in covers on the side of the bed. I heard a low, soft whimpering sound coming from him and definitely knew it was time for me to be gone. I backed out of the room to get one last look at Lisa as I closed the door behind me.

As soon as I was out of the room and walking toward the elevators, I saw Shirley, Bill's oldest sister, I think. She was coming right toward me. I couldn't remember whether Shirley or the other one was the oldest, but I did remember meeting her over the years at Lisa's house. Shirley was moving quickly in my direction, and as I looked up, our eyes met. She was literally standing inches away from me. She reached out and gave me a big bear hug! Shirley was a big woman, not fat but just overall big. The word *Amazon* came to mind when I thought about her.

"How are you doing?" she asked as she squeezed me in her Amazonian arms, my face buried in her breast.

I tried to say, "Not good," but it came out more like "No could." I don't know if she heard, but at that moment, she squeezed me even tighter.

Finally, after several seconds, she released me from her embrace and stared at me intently, looking me over from head to toe. The grief of the situation was evident in her face as she looked as if she had been crying. She saw my pain and her eyes filled with water.

"You know, Thomas, I always liked you," she finally said once she had regained her composure. She tilted her head back and to the right and stared into my face as if she was seeking some unspoken acknowledgment. I wanted to tell her how much I loved her brother's wife and that Lisa was more than just a friend, that our friendship was a weird kind of life dance of two people too in love to disappoint the other, that we never found the courage to try, to explore the real nature of our feelings. But I couldn't. These thoughts were my burden to bear, and I definitely couldn't share them with the sister of

Lisa's husband, no matter how comfortable she made me feel.

I said nothing in response as I just stood there looking at her. Something inside of me said that she knew, or that she suspected, that over the years she saw some interaction between us that betrayed us. But if she did, she never said anything, never challenged her thoughts by testing them with questions designed to seek out the truth.

"You take care of yourself, and I will pray for you, Thomas. It's good seeing you again, but I do regret the circumstances," she said as she tried to smile. But her face wouldn't cooperate, not exactly the best situation for things like smiles and reunion-style happy hugs. I couldn't explain it, but I truly appreciated her empathy and the way she was trying to be supportive. She hugged me again but less tightly this time. "You take of yourself, OK?" she said a second time as she released me from her embrace.

"I will," I said responding weakly as I felt the grief rising in me again, brought on by Lisa's sister-in-law's authentic effort to comfort me. She looked as if she wanted to say more and have that conversation people who haven't seen each other in a long time have, but she sensed that it wouldn't happen. So she just said, "I'll see you soon."

We would talk one more time before I left Norfolk, but that talk would be even more depressing and heartbreaking. I was relieved that the encounter was over so I could be left in my grief as the tears started to flow again and I felt guilty for crying in public and thought that this guilt probably had something to do with my childhood and my interpretation of manhood.

As I walked out of the hospital, the air hit my uncovered face and chilled my body. I shivered and shook even though I was wearing a coat suited for cold, winter weather. Being outside distracted me momentarily from my current grief. The wind was blowing, and it made the cool air even colder. It was dark, but the city lights made the darkness bearable. I felt like a character in that remade movie about the creature found in ice at the North Pole that could possess a person's body to survive, and the crew had to figure out who carried the creature and who didn't. In the end, the last two characters found themselves outside while buildings burned. They sat staring at each other, not sure if the other was possessed. The wind blew in their faces as they tried to stay warm. I never knew whether they survived or not, but what I remembered was how cold and frozen they looked as the wind and snow violently blew all around them, and I remembered how they had completely accepted their hopeless situation because there was nothing they could do to change it. And that's exactly how I felt: cold and utterly hopeless in a situation that I was powerless to change.

Each time the wind gusted, my body shivered, and I could have turned around and walked back into the warmth of the hospital but I didn't. I looked around and spotted a bench off to my left and walked over and sat down. My winter coat was adequate, but I was still cold and uncomfortable. I pulled the phone from my pocket and called my sister. No one answered, and I left a message telling her where I was and that I needed a ride. I put the phone back in my pocket and sat there quietly, watching the cold, white air as it left my nose and sometimes my mouth, feeling my chest rising and falling as I breathed. I was convinced the temperature was dropping by the minute, but I was not motivated in the slightest to move and seek the warmth inside of the hospital. I just sat there, waiting and not knowing when my sister would appear, and I was perfectly OK to be on the bench, not motivated to do anything beyond simply existing.

And so, I sat there quietly, my arms folded across my chest in an effort to stay warm, lost in my own misery and self-pity.

We don't always have all of the
information we need to make
decisions in life, so we use what
we have, make the best ones that
we can, and hope for the best.

I didn't call anyone the next morning and had my sister drop me off on her way to work. She had to be at work by six in the morning, and she lived forty minutes from her office. That reality put me at the hospital at five thirty, and I wasn't sure if I would be allowed to see Lisa so early in the morning. If I was unfortunate enough to be too early for visiting hours, then I resigned myself to wait in the waiting room.

The whole drop-off had a comforting feeling of déjà vu, reminding me of the times I was dropped off at Norfolk State. When I was in college, I remember being dropped off at the bus station and sometimes at college in the wee hours of the morning. Some days I arrived just after the janitorial staff opened the buildings and I would wait in the lobby until the building came to life with other students, instructors, workers, and all those who worked to make the machine called higher education run. I used this time to get in some last-minute studying, especially if I was taking an exam that day.

My academic prudence worked until a young lady named Claudette started showing up ten minutes after my arrival. She obviously had the same transportation arrangement as me and so we started talking and became early morning companions. Claudette was fun and easy to talk to, although I often found myself wondering how good of a student she was. On the rare occasions when we talked about test scores and studying for exams, Claudette sounded like she was a stone's throw away from being on academic probation, and my theory was reinforced when we got comfortable enough to plan a date.

The last time I saw Claudette that school year, she told me that her dad had grown tired of dropping her off in the mornings, so he bought her a car. So we had planned a date and she would come to pick me up from my sister's house. I loved her liberated thinking of picking up a man who didn't have a car and was basically walking and borrowing cars to get around. But unfortunately, ole Claudette never made it to the house that night of our date, and when I called her that same night to see what happened, she said she got lost, then she got confused and frustrated and finally gave up altogether in trying to find me. I didn't know whether that was the truth or just a story she told me after having a change of heart, but I found the whole story completely believable after having spent almost an entire semester meeting her in the early morning hours and talking about school, life, and just being young.

As I entered the main lobby of the hospital, I noticed that no one was at the front desk, and I wondered if the young, white girl who was so helpful yesterday was working. With no one to check in and no one to stop me, I headed to the elevator on my way to see Lisa.

As I stepped off the elevator, I could see Bill, his sister, and a few others near the door to Lisa's room. Everyone was standing but Bill. Everyone was crying, and Bill was making a God-awful wailing sound like someone was beating a walrus, and it was the saddest, most depressing thing I had ever heard coming from the insides of a person.

I could feel the emotion rise in me as approached the group. When I got there, Bill was sitting in a chair someone had dragged into the hall. Actually, he was more slumped over than sitting, his face staring at the floor, and he was crying that uncontrollable walrus-beating cry. Everyone else seemed to be attempting to console Bill as he repeated over and over, "She's gone. She's gone …"

I looked from face to face to face and saw only crying and sadness. I walked over and looked inside the room where I had seen Lisa last night. The room was empty, the bed had been made as if no one had been there just a few hours earlier, and my pain was now tinged with traces of anger at Bill and myself. I blamed myself for leaving that night and Bill for whatever happened, that allowed the room to be empty, that allowed Lisa to be taken away when I left.

Shirley walked over to me, and I don't know what she saw in my face, but she looked both sad and worried. She grabbed and hugged me, and my whole body started to shake uncontrollably. I felt lightheaded and weak. Her embrace steadied me, and she held me until the fainting sensation passed.

"She passed away earlier this morning," she whispered in my ear as she held me tightly in that Amazonian embrace. "She's gone to a better place, Thomas."

I was angry at Bill for allowing her to die and even more upset with myself for leaving last night. "I should have stayed," I finally said.

"There was nothing you could have done."

"I could have said goodbye. I could have held her hand one last time, and I could have kissed her and said a proper goodbye. I could have said that I was sorry for not being the man I should have been when she needed me to be."

Shirley didn't respond because there really was nothing left to say. This was not a time for any more words or discussions about what happened and what people did or didn't do. It was only a time for tears, regret, loss, and sadness.

After what seemed like hours, the group found strength to move on down the hall toward the elevators. Bill was being carried like a reluctant inmate headed for the electric chair. Shirley held up one side and some man I didn't recognize held the other. They looked to be dragging him more than he was walking, and he was still making that dying walrus sound.

My anger started to slowly leave me as I watched this pitiful sight of a man completely devastated by the untimely death of his beautiful wife. I always knew he genuinely loved her, even when he screwed up doing stupid guy stuff. Lisa's death had broken something in me, but it had destroyed Bill's very being. He had overcome his immature mistakes from the earlier days of their relationship, and during those early years, she had either forgiven him or accepted the fact that she loved an idiot. In the end, he had lost her love and her respect. And I wondered still if she ever really loved him. I had no answers and there would never be an opportunity to get any. I had always believed that regardless of the paths our lives took, we would always find a way back to each other and stay connected until our olden days, when we would share stories sitting on a porch, remembering all the things we did when we were young, beautiful, and amazing.

As the family left the hospital floor, I was still standing by the door of Lisa's room, not knowing quite what to do next and lost in my own grief. Shirley returned a few minutes later and asked if I needed her to stay. Then she tried to share information about when the funeral would possibly happen, and I listened half-heartedly.

"I'm worried about you, Thomas," she said, looking at me through strained, bloodshot eyes from too little sleep and too much crying.

"I'll be fine," I responded, my face soaked from a steady stream of tears that ran down my cheeks and into my mouth.

She gave me one final, loving hug, and then she was gone again, and the next time I would see Shirley was at Lisa's funeral. But we would never get a chance to speak to each other again.

As soon as I heard the elevators close, I went back into Lisa's room and sat in the same chair I was in that night when I was next to her bed. I lovingly touched the part of the bed where her head had been. Then I kissed the pillow before I pulled it from the covers and placed it in my lap. I lifted it to my face, feeling its softness, and then I cried even harder as I buried my face in it. I cried for everything that would never be, and I lamented over the complete and utter lack of control I had over everything that was happening and how unfair and unjust it all felt.

After what seemed like hours, but was only minutes, that same nurse I had talked to briefly the day before, popped her head at the door, looking both surprised and curious at the same time. Realizing that the room was occupied when it should have been empty, she knocked three times as she walked into the room. I looked up at her as she stared at me with an expression I can only describe as pity and then she proceeded to pull the chair on the far side of the bed next to mine. I was not in the mood for any more words of comfort, and I really wanted to be left alone in my grief.

She placed her chair as close to mine as she could get, the two chairs almost touching each other, and then she reached over and put her arm around my shoulder. The old school part of me didn't want to be seen crying in the presence of the pretty, young nurse, but emotional regulation left me as soon as I heard that Lisa had passed away. She held me and I found myself leaning into her arms as I cried. We both sat there, and to my surprise, she didn't say a word the whole time. She let me cry until I could gain some semblance of emotional control again. I expected her to start trying to politely and empathetically usher me out of the room, but she didn't seem to be in any hurry and made no effort to hurry me out.

"In all the rushing and the commotion of everything, I don't even know what happened to her except that she was in a comatose state yesterday and now she is gone," I said, finally finding the strength to speak.

"No one from her family told you what happened?" she asked, somewhat surprised that I knew so little.

"I don't know if there was time since everything happened so fast and everyone was too busy grieving," I said.

"Oh," she responded.

"Everyone you saw here was from her husband's side of the family. I don't know why her dad didn't come, but I thought I would have plenty of time to hear the details once she recovered. Well, I just thought I had more time to understand everything," I continued.

"I see," she responded. "It's not my place to tell you cause you ain't direct family, but she was in a car accident, and she didn't die from the accident because when EMT was called they heard her talking in the background. They said she was complaining of head and chest pains and that her arm and the right side of her body was hurting. At least that's what the nurses in the emergency room said. She was hit from behind by another car right out in front of their house, and they were talking to the driver of the other car. Between that conversation and the police arriving, she went down, and by the time the police and EMS showed up, she was lying on the ground unconscious. Her husband was lost in hysteria, sitting on the ground with her head in his lap. The 911 operator was still on the phone and was trying to tell Bill what to do, but he was in total panic mode and must have put the phone on the hood of the car when she fell cause that's where they found it when they arrived."

She paused to see if I had any comments or responses to what she had just told me. Hearing nothing, she continued.

"The EMS guy told the emergency room nurse that if he had just tried to administer CPR then she had a good chance of survival, that she was young enough and strong enough that she could have made it. But that's one man's opinion. People always say that woulda, coulda stuff after the fact."

When she stopped speaking, I said nothing because there was just nothing else left to say. Then the polite nudge came, and she said, "You can stay here a few more minutes, but we will need this room soon for a patient coming out of surgery."

I wanted to tell her how grateful I was for her compassion and understanding and for telling me what happened, even though she was breaking a hospital rule, but when I finally opened my mouth, only two words came out. "Thank you."

"Welcome," she said as she got up and left the room. She closed the door behind her as she left to give me a few more minutes to get myself together before some big orderly would show up and hustle me out.

I looked around the room one last time but couldn't find the strength or courage to leave. This was the last place I saw her alive, the last place I touched her and felt her presence. A part of me always wanted to believe that she would recover fully, that she would be that miracle, and that I would maybe get a second chance to say all the things I should have said a long time ago, a last chance to try and make things right between us.

I thought about the last missed window of opportunity when she caught Bill cheating or trying to cheat or whatever the hell he was trying to do. This happened shortly after I had graduated and was starting my work on a master's degree before I decided that I just couldn't do another two or three years in college and gave up that pursuit. I had a small apartment just north of campus. Lisa called me one evening either on a Friday or Saturday and was frantic. I heard a tenseness in her voice that I had never heard before and she asked if I could pick her up from campus. I was at first confused as she had a car and could just as easily drive herself.

"Can you come right now and pick me up?" she said over the phone, more like a command than a request.

Again, a strange request to me, because Lisa knew I had an old car that went nowhere quickly. The heat never went completely off. It drank way too much gas, and the passenger side door didn't open from the inside. So, I started to ask if she could pick me up since she had the nicer car and that I would drive her car, but my mind guy that feeds my thoughts yelled, "Don't do it!" So I said, "I'm on my way."

I pulled up into the U-shaped driveway in front of the dorm about twenty minutes later, and she was standing out front. As soon as my car reached her and before I could come to a complete stop, Lisa was climbing into the car. I looked over at her and saw nothing but a determined, focused look on her face. As I looked at her, she stared straight forward, never turned my way and totally dispensed with the perfunctory hello and "How are you doing?" talk.

"We need to go now, and we need to hurry," she said, and this time the tone in her voice was definitely a command. *I can do one but not the other. I can drive now but I can't hurry. If you want a car that could hurry, then we should be taking your car on this mysterious mission.* I thought this while I pulled out of the driveway but was not crazy enough

220

to verbalize these thoughts. Lisa was angry and I still didn't know where we were going or why she was so upset. So I decided to just shut up and drive and hoped that she wouldn't get pissed off at me for the lack of the "hurry" part of the trip.

We drove in silence as she stared directly forward during the entire trip that took a little more than thirty minutes. As we turned into Pittman Street, I noticed that we were traveling to Bill's side of town, and I started to feel a little nervous. An angry black woman going to her boyfriend's house was the beginning of every bad movie gone wrong. I could just see myself telling the police, "And then she just stabbed him right in the heart with a knife that came out of nowhere."

Once we arrived on Pitman Street, we were only two houses down from the brick frame bungalow that Bill called home. As we approached the house, Lisa said in a low, menacing voice that angry women go to "keep going." Now I was completely lost as to where we were going because my original destination that I thought wasn't where we were going now, yet another sign that nothing happening on this fateful evening was going to turn out well. We drove for another mile and half, and the neighborhood transitioned from neat, tidy, single-family homes to multifamily apartments and then to commercial buildings.

"Turn at the corner," Lisa said.

As we rounded the corner, we were clearly in a commercial area as the traditional businesses appeared on both side of the road: McDonald's, a law office, a gas station on each side of the street, and all the usual stores and businesses found on every commercial corridor in any city USA.

About midblock I saw an Economy Lodge motel sign. Then Lisa said, "Turn into the motel," and all I could think was *Oh shit*. At this point, even the village idiot could figure out what was about to happen. "You think this is a good idea?" I found myself saying.

"Go down to the end of this row," Lisa said as if I hadn't said a word.

So I went on down to the end of the row, and before the car came to a complete stop, Lisa jumped out and headed toward the back of my car. Rounding the back, she turned right and then left and dashed down the breezeway. I was absolutely amazed at how fast she moved, especially since she had to reach out the window and open the door from the outside. And when did she roll down the window? I missed that move completely!

When the car came to a complete stop, I was sitting in the middle of a row, my passenger door wide open, trying to process what had just happened as Lisa had just rounded the back of my car like a baseball player rounding a base. She was moving faster than I thought she was capable of moving. I guess she had decided that I was taking too long or that I would ruin the element of surprise because she disappeared around a corner at the end of the hallway. She was moving so fast she almost flipped a laundry cart that popped out on her as she ran down the walkway.

"Damn," I said to myself as I climbed out the driver's side of the car to close the door she'd left open. I knew I should have been moving with a little more urgency since now I had to figure out where she disappeared to, but thinking and moving faster were two different things. And quite frankly, I wasn't sure what my role was in this type of situation.

Once back in the car, I turned left and headed in the direction I saw Lisa go. I rounded another corner as I tracked her path. I didn't see her anywhere so I decided to park and look for her on foot. The first thought that crossed my mind was *What if she went into one of the rooms and the door closed? How the hell will I find out where she went and what is happening in that room?*

The thought of not being able to find my best friend started to freak me out. But that issue was put to rest because, as I walked back toward the motel from the parking lot and toward the rooms on the north side of the building, I heard some incomprehensible yelling and screaming. The noise was coming from a unit well down the corridor, and I found myself once again amazed at how far Lisa had run in such a short period of time. At that point I started to move with a little more urgency.

As I approached the room, the door was partially open, and I could see a person's back and a leg sticking out, and it was going in and out like one of those Whac-a-Moles and someone was trying to close the door from the inside. Everything in me wanted to laugh because it looked funny.

When I finally stood closer to the room entrance, the leg, a torso, and a head were trying to back out of the room, and I realized that it was Bill doing the Whac-a-Mole next to the door. He was involved in a sort of bizarre tug-of-war with someone deeper in the room. The yelling had stopped, and the pulling back and forth had gotten even more intense.

When my view allowed me to look deeper into the room, I saw that Lisa was on the other end of the tug-a-war competition and she was trying to tear away from Bill's one-arm grasp and pulling fiercely to free herself. She was using the door as leverage as she attempted to smash him with it using her free arm and her shoulder as Bill yanked on her other arm, but Bill was winning as she was slowly and defiantly being pulled out of the hotel room. Then she let go of the door and started to use the free hand to punch Bill in any part of his exposed body that she could reach. She was landing blow after blow on his arm and shots to his face when he mistakenly leaned in too close.

I watched all of this unfold with feelings of both shock and amusement. Then I heard the grunting and punching noises as Lisa fought viciously to free her arm and Bill held on desperately, taking blow after blow after blow. Bill was in a strong tug-a-war stance with good leverage, but he could only use one arm to pull and so had no ability to properly shield himself now that Lisa was hitting him with the free hand. All he could do was to move up and down and slightly from side to side to protect himself from the barrage of shots.

I was again amazed and baffled that Lisa had somehow gotten all the way into the room in the first place. I knew I should have been doing something to stop this fight, but I honestly didn't know what exactly to do. Bill was on the receiving end of the violence as she was now jabbing the hell out of his face as she was trying to pull away from him. The whole scene looked like something out of one of those romantic comedies gone wrong. Bill was bobbing and weaving even more now as the shots turned into a continuous barrage of jabs, upper cuts, and wide roundabout punches to the side of his face when he moved too slowly or in the wrong direction. She would swing and miss, then he would try to anticipate her next shot, and it was at that point that she would pop him with one of those jabs in the face.

"Stop it, Lisa!" Bill started yelling, but to no avail.

Bill leaned in one too many times and slightly lost his firm stance as one of his legs slipped. He was now in a completely defenseless position and Lisa was scoring direct hit after hit, and the only good thing Bill was doing was deflecting a direct shot to the balls. He tried to protect himself by maneuvering his body into a sideways position and turning his face away and downward, but the periodic licks kept ruining his defense timing and he had to decide each time whether to take a punch in the face or take a direct hit to the nuts. He tried to recover from the slip that had weakened his stance because now he was in jeopardy of falling. It may have been my overactive imagination, but I thought I could literally see his face swelling with each direct hit that Lisa landed on it. That evil side of me and my American overstimulation to violence told me to do nothing and just watch. Lisa was really winning now and was in no danger as Bill struggled to improve his position to reduce his chance of going down. He just kept trying to pull her out of the room and avoid as many punches as he could. He managed to recover slightly as he shifted his right leg position, and for a moment he looked to have recovered enough because

Lisa was once again being pulled out, but Bill was paying a painfully high price for his efforts. During the drama he turned quickly to the right and looked up as if to say something and to avoid another lick, and just like clockwork, Lisa jabbed the hell out of him with her free hand, landing a shot directly on the side of his nose. Blood trickled down his face. As he turned away, we made eye contact. A momentary sense of relief filled his face.

"Help me with your gir—"

Then boom! Another shot in the face. Lisa increased her offensive attack, focusing exclusively on Bill's head and face, delivering shots in rapid succession as the barrage finally forced him to loosen his grip on her arm. She started jabbing him repeatedly directly in the face. The continuous shots forced Bill to let go of her arm right as he had her almost completely out of the room. That final barrage of punches sent Bill backward into the breezeway, and as soon as Lisa was free, she instantly disappeared deeper into the room and out of my view for a few seconds.

My first thought was to follow her into the room, to go after her and to try to prevent anything else she was about to do. After that I heard a loud scream and a door slam as a white sheer dress disappeared into what I could only guess was the bathroom. I walked slowly, deeper into the hotel room, and found myself standing in the middle of one of those living room spaces of a motel suite. I watched in awe as Lisa reached that closed bathroom door just seconds after it slammed shut in her face. She was inches away from grabbing that skirt, dress, lingerie, or whatever it was that the other woman was wearing. I found myself thanking the Lord that woman was just fast enough to make into the room.

Lisa slammed into the door with her left shoulder just as it closed and it didn't give a single inch, which told me that the lingerie lady was leaning on that door as soon as she was in and locked it after Lisa's initial impact. That scene also told me that there was a very good chance that she was a big girl because Lisa hit that door on the move and even with her momentum, she didn't get that door to move a single inch! Big girl. That goofy Bill was trying to have an affair with a big girl less than two miles from his own house! Dumbass!

"Bring your ass out here!" Lisa screamed as the realization hit her that she was not going to get into that bathroom. She yelled it multiple times, but no response from the other side of the door.

As I walked where Lisa was standing, I was still searching for the right thing to say and do. People think about what should be said in critical moments, but in real life, we usually never find the right words for the big moments. All I had was the same thing I said earlier. "You sure you want to do this, Lisa?"

She paused and looked directly at me, and as she stared, she seemed to be looking through me. It was one of those moments when a person looks right at you and they are not seeing you; their eyes are just looking at you, but their mind is in another universe. There was a craziness, a wildness in her face that I had never seen before and never saw again. The stare was brief and probably only lasted for a moment, but I felt like it lasted a small eternity.

Then her expression changed slightly. "You right. I'm talking to the wrong damn person," she finally said and headed right toward me.

For a minute, I was completely confused as she was coming toward me, and I was trying to figure out why I was now the person she needed to talk to. Duh! She wasn't talking about me, and she walked past me like I wasn't even there. I turned as she passed me, expecting Bill to be somewhere in the room near the door, but he wasn't. Bill was nowhere to be seen. Lisa was walking fast, and then she started running as soon as she got to the motel room door.

After a few seconds, I heard what sounded like someone hitting something, and then I heard her yelling for Bill to get out of the car. No, that negro was not trying to leave the scene of his relationship crime!

"Let me go, Lisa!" Bill screamed.

"Get out the car!" Lisa responded again.

At that point, I was completely clueless about what to do next. The naughty by nature part of my personality told me to stay in the room so I could see what the other woman looked like, but the situation outside sounded more dire.

"Let go of my neck!" I heard Bill yell.

And it was followed by the same response from Lisa. "Get out of the car!"

I was trying to create a visual in my mind of what was happening, and the smarter part of me said, "You'd better go out there before somebody gets hurt."

As I reached the doorway of the room, I looked back briefly to see if the woman was coming out of the bathroom, still hoping that I would see a glance of Bill's partner in this relationship crime, but I saw nothing but a closed bathroom door and not a single sound came from inside. As I turned, I saw Lisa and Bill in the parking lot only two doors down from that room I had just left. "Oh shit!" was my reaction.

Lisa was trying to pull Bill through the driver's side window headfirst. He was screaming as he was trying to get free. "Let me go! Let me the fuck go," he said desperately, but Lisa was completely unfazed by his profanity or pleas.

After that last plea, Lisa attempted to walk away from the car with Bill's head in her vise grip arms, and Bill gagged uncontrollably.

I quickly ran over to the car and tried to remove Lisa's arms from around Bill's neck. I was able to push her back closer to the car to relieve that neck pressure on Bill. Lisa had locked one arm across the other like that wrestling move you see on TV just before someone taps out or passes out. Frankly, I was shocked how tight the grip was around Bill's neck as he was now clawing her arms, especially her right arm that seemed to be doing the most damage. So that was also the arm I targeted, and I pulled desperately to free him of the death grip. I was absolutely amazed at how strong the grip was. The thought of superhuman women pulling cars off babies came to mind.

It took both of us to get Lisa's arms from around Bill's neck. When I finally set him free, Bill dropped back into the car and Lisa and I fell backward. I lost my balance and Lisa's entire 142 pounds landed right on top of me as I hit the hard concrete. Pain shot up my right leg and all the way up my back to the base of my neck. For a moment, I was afraid to move. Then I heard the car engine start up and watched as Bill backed out of the parking space.

Lisa seemed to be momentarily stunned by the fall as the back of her head hit me in the face. But when she saw the car moving, she started to get up, but I grabbed her and held on. Fighting next to a parked car was very different from fighting while a car was moving. And I don't know whether it was dumb luck or just Bill paying attention to where we landed on the ground, but we were still pretty close to his car. We fell back and away so we were parallel with the car as it backed out. But Bill turned the car's front wheels away from us as he proceeded to leave the scene. Lisa struggled to get free, and when I saw that we were out of danger of being run over, I was about to let her go when she elbowed me in the nose! The pain was instant and excruciating and I immediately let go.

She popped up, and for a moment I thought she was going to chase the car, but she just stood there watching as it left the parking lot. Then she looked toward the room and then she looked down at me. Her facial features started to soften.

"You're bleeding," she finally said.

I touched my nose and felt the warm blood. Then she knelt and proceeded to help me up. I groaned in agony as she slowly and carefully pulled me up from the ground.

Once on my feet, I noticed that this Jerry Springer-style experience had drawn a crowd. Random faces were staring from the parking lot, from motel windows, and from onlookers from the walkway. No one said anything; they just looked at us as if they had been watching a show. I saw a few smiles, smirks, and looks of surprise, but all my mind could focus on was the pain in my back and leg and the blood on my face.

Lisa put my arm over her shoulder, and I winced in pain. A part of me wanted to cry, but there were too many spectators, and I didn't want to cry in front of Lisa, the person who was responsible for my current raggedy situation. We walked together slowly and gingerly toward my car. I could feel the stares as we moved away from the motel and into the parking lot. As we passed the infamous room, I noticed that the door was closed, most likely locked and thus officially ending this drama as there was nothing to do but leave.

Bill was gone, his partner in crime locked in a motel room, and I needed medical care. And after all the drama, I was the one who suffered the most, assuming that Lisa hadn't damaged Bill's neck when she tried to pull his head off.

There was just something about this whole situation that didn't seem to be fair to me. Maybe it was my karma for not being more helpful and in a sick kind of a way enjoying how Lisa was beating the hell out of Bill. I guess I did enjoy the whole crazy soap opera experiences, and now my punishment was to bleed to death in my own car while going home or being forever deformed from a fall that probably permanently ruined my back. I should have been more empathic and timelier in being helpful when everything was happening so quickly.

We rode home on that day and didn't talk at all, and I could see the changes in Lisa's facial expressions as she thought about everything that happened. She appeared to be struggling between anger, pain, and disappointment, always on the verge of crying, but something hardened inside of her that prevented her from crying.

In that processing, I wondered if she was aware how strong her ass was when she was truly pissed off. Deep down I thought that her relationship with Bill was forever over and that if I survived my injuries, I would be there to support her and help her through this difficult time. Again, I admit that comfort and support were none of my positive attributes, but neither of us was native to Virginia, and right now I was all she had.

After I got back to my place, Lisa stayed until I was comfortably lying on my couch and my bleeding had stopped. She even went out and picked up some Chinese food, all my favorites. I think it was guilt food and her way of saying that she was sorry for what happened to me, but I didn't care. Free food was free food, and when you're a transitioning college student with very little money, any free food was good food.

I told her that she could stay if she didn't want to be alone, but she said that she needed to think and that it was better if she went home for that. She asked to borrow my car until the next day, and seeing how it was useless in my current condition, I handed over the keys to my only real possession in the world. She kissed me on the forehead and gave me one of her beautiful, loving smiles as she closed the front door and leaving me to recover.

I saw a side of Lisa that excited and terrified me at the same time, and I was so glad that I was not the brunt of her anger. I realized that day that there is something to that "woman scorned" thing.

I turned too quickly to get the TV remote, and pain shot all through my body, so I laid flat on my back looking sideways at the TV until I fell asleep.

Our thoughts often betray us in matters of the heart. We find ourselves creating amazing relationships that oftentimes only exist in our dreams and fantasies.

I had always believed that from the drama of that day a relationship would blossom between Lisa and me and it would finally have a space to be explored, that we would finally see each other and say things that needed to be said, but that didn't happen at all. She casually told me later that she was talking to Bill the very same day that she had choked him out. Bill wound up in the emergency room that day because of his neck injuries, and I'm not sure if her guilt did not drive that initial conversation.

Somehow, they started talking, and the talking led to a reconciliation of that relationship, and she was once again hanging out at his house, probably helping him recover as he did need one of those giant-looking plastic neck braces that won't allow a person to turn their head. I remember seeing him after that motel day and he reminded me of one of those dogs forced to wear that funnel-looking device to keep them from scratching their ass or something like that.

Shortly after the fight, she was practically living there again as if nothing had ever happened. And it was this realization that I knew I would never understand women, that she did seem to love him then, even despite his pathetic effort to get side booty at a motel less than two miles from his own house!

It was at that point that our relationship changed forever in my mind as I finally thought that I had let go of the fear of being rejected as a soulmate. A part of me knew that she was the closest thing I had come to finding the true-life companion but that we would forever be endearing friends. I couldn't name the feeling but knew something inside of me changed the way I saw relationships and how I related to all women. My mind had remembered the situation as a missed opportunity, and I had carried that misguided thought around for years. In actuality, there was no space for us at that time, only the drama of a woman in love dealing with a cheating boyfriend who was bad at it. I always was just a spectator, that steady friend always being what she needed when she needed me, and she had always been the same for me, an eternal, sincere, caring, listening friend.

Grief and death have a way of stripping away all pretenses of who we think we are or what we are. For years I thought I had turned the corner but being at the hospital brought all of the pain, anguish, and disappointment back like a reoccurring cancer whose only gifts are pain, suffering, and in many cases eventual death. I contemplated this as I sat. For years I thought I was over her and that I had accepted our relationship. My mind told me that even if I told her how I really felt, it wouldn't have mattered, and nothing would have changed. I still found myself regretting that I never found the courage to say what should have been said. Now she was gone, and I knew that I would never stop missing her, that I would have to live with regret. I wanted to believe that she loved me as much as I loved her, but now I would never know for sure. Maybe she could have explained our relationship in a way that made sense to me, why she made the decision to marry Bill, and if she loved him or just needed him at that point in her life—or that we were victims of poor timing.

I would have accepted anything she said after she confirmed that she loved me too. Her relationship with Bill just didn't make any reasonable sense to me. He fulfilled or completed something in her that she needed at that stage in her life, something that I couldn't. I decided that I was going to try harder to move on from all of the what-if thoughts that would not change the finality of our relationship but I still found myself wishing we had that last conversation because her love for her husband was over when we last spoke and I couldn't help but believe that the opportunity we had waited a lifetime for was about to unfold, and it's that possibility that torments my thoughts and dreams. Now I am forced to face the sad reality that whatever we had or didn't have, it was over forever and nothing in this world could change that truth.

I put the pillow back on the bed next to the two others. I shook it and tried to fluff it up so that it would look like the other ones, after I used it to wipe my face. I rose to my feet and casually rubbed my hand along the side of the bed. The sun was shining through the window as both curtains were pulled to each side and tied off. I hadn't really noticed when I first entered the room that the sunlight was coming through the window and resting in the center of the bed. The moment filled me with a sense of sadness. "I still really hate hospitals," I said to myself.

And then I headed out the room, down the elevator, out of the hospital, and back into a world that felt less loving and more indifferent to the whims of people and their petty problems and emotions. My mind swirled around the hospital visit trying to make sense of the event, but the thoughts started to be clouded with fragments and pieces of other random mental pictures, and there was always that nonsense person like one of my ex-girlfriends standing in a hallway with changing faces or some random woman looking through the window, with a face I couldn't clearly see, and my mind would tell me it was Claudette and not Charlene and those random thoughts distorted the flow of the dreams.

"Thomas, Thomas, Thomas." I heard this faintly like someone was whispering in my ear.

The darkness started to subside slowly. I could now see the vague glimmer of light, and the thoughts and mental pictures of the hospital visit faded back in the recesses of my mind. I knew I would remember little of the thoughts once I was fully in the light of consciousness.

I awoke and realized that I was in a sitting position with my back pressed against the front driver side of Andrea's SUV. She was leaning over me, her face only inches from my own, a frightened, terrified look covering her face. When I could focus enough to make eye contact, her facial expression instantly changed, and she attempted to hug me as best as she could in my seated position.

"Damn, you scared the hell out me. For a minute, I thought you had had a heart attack of something." Her words filled with the sound of relief from someone who had just averted some great catastrophe.

She leaned back and just stared at me, smiling broadly because I was still among the living. And I just stared back, not knowing where I was, why I was on the ground, and why we were in what looked like a cemetery.

Watching my less than focused behavior, she said, "You OK, Thomas? Cause you look really confused."

I still could only just stare and wonder because my mental mind guy was somewhere, and I couldn't process or remember anything, so I just sat, stared, and listened. Seeing my bewilderment, Andrea decided to give me a recap of what had recently happened to explain why I was sitting on the ground in a graveyard, staring out at a world that appeared foreign to me.

"You fell, Thomas, after you answered a phone call on your cell phone," she said in an effort to refresh my memory. She paused as if to ask, "Now don't you remember?" Then she leaned in closer. "And you hit your head apparently when you fell face-first in the grass." She stepped back and said, "I'll be right back." She stood up and disappeared around the truck.

My senses were the only thing working as I continued to look out into an unfamiliar world. I now was feeling the cold ground under my butt, and I heard the car door open and close. I tried hard to remember, to mentally process what was happening, but my mind was as empty as a sweet potato tray on Thanksgiving.

After a few moments, Andrea returned with a small kit with a red cross on the cover. She set it next to me on the ground and removed some different-shaped bandages. She stared at my forehead and looked at two sizes. Then she took a napkin from her pocket and wiped the left side of my forehead. As she set the napkin on the ground, she took out a small bottle of liquid and put some on another napkin and wiped my head again. Red blood formed a Rorschach pattern on the first napkin, and it took me a minute to realize that the blood belonged to me! I immediately felt a sharp pain as the liquid douched on the second napkin was pressed against me forehead.

"You're bleeding, but it doesn't look too bad," she said as she administered first aid. As she said this, she placed a square bandage on my head and pressed the corners to ensure that it would stick, and she leaned back again to get a better look at her handiwork and seemed pleased with her effort. I still sat there like the village idiot, saying nothing but feeling everything around me.

"Let's get you up and back in the car," she said, seemingly satisfied that everything was OK again.

"OK," I heard myself say, surprised by the sound of my own voice.

She grabbed my arm and I braced myself with my hands to get up from a spot that was getting colder by the minute, and until I figured out what had happened, I knew that a warm SUV was definitely better than a cold seat on the ground. My head started to hurt as soon as I got into a standing position, and my balance was

off as I tried to walk. I was forced to
lean into Andrea, putting more of my
weight on her smaller frame than I felt
comfortable doing, but she held it and
steadied me enough to walk me around to
the passenger side of her car. My steps
were the measured movement of a drunk as I
drifted uncontrollably from side to side,
and Andrea was forced to pull me in when
I wanted to fall away and then steady me
again when my weight shifted as she walked
me over the short distance.

Before she dumped me into the seat, she
tried to brush off as much of the dirt and
other debris that I had collected from
my nosedive into dirtville. I fell into
the front seat more than I sat and then
pulled myself into a seated position as she
rounded the Navigator to get into her own.

"You think we should go to the
hospital?" she said, the concern and
anxiety apparent in her voice.

"No, I'll be all right in a minute,"
I said in response, again surprised at
hearing my own voice.

Andrea stared at me as if to say, "You
don't look all right."

"My mind is a little cloudy, but it will
clear up in a minute," I said in response.
"I just need a little time", I continued,
hoping that my words would assure her that
we were ready to get back on the road and
no hospital visit so far from home was
needed.

I had never passed out and fallen on my face before, but I had been knocked unconscious in a high school football game and some of the effects from that impact felt very similar to what I was experiencing now.

We sat there for a moment while Andrea decided if I was telling the truth or if she was just going to drive me to a hospital anyway. And based on the way I was feeling, I didn't really have the energy or motivation to even care, and encouraging words on my condition were all I had to offer because I wasn't sure just what my overall wellness was. My head was throbbing, and I couldn't remember what had happened beyond me sitting on the ground. I couldn't even remember what time of the day it was. I wanted so desperately to look down at my watch on my arm but was afraid that that action would send the wrong signal.

"Let's go home," I finally said to break the silence, even though I had no idea where home was.

And I guess that's what she was waiting to hear because she quickly started the big SUV, the engine roared to life and easily settled into that smooth, expensive truck idle, and we moved down the narrow driveway. We made a sharp right out of the cemetery and back onto an asphalt road, and I found myself wondering, *What were we doing in a cemetery?*

Rick Tenmoo

"You still don't remember, Thomas?" Andrea said, the concern even more obvious in her tone.

I didn't want her to start the whole hospital thing again and realized that I had actually asked the question out loud when I thought I was just thinking it in my head. "It's not completely clear, but some of it is slowly coming back to me," I said.

A part of me felt bad about the lie, but I just wanted to go home, wherever home was, and I hoped that I would be OK in a few minutes, but I just needed to keep the conversation simple enough to not upset my driver.

The big SUV moved easily through multiple subdivisions with large, expensive-looking houses with manicured lawns and at least two cars in each driveway. I sat quietly, trying to look out the window as if I was observing something important that needed my attention.

We rode in silence for about thirty minutes. Then we passed a small church that appeared to be surrounded by cars, and when we got closer, I noticed the "Just married" sign on the door of a black Camaro sitting directly in front of the front entrance of the church. Someone was getting married. And then my mind was filled with a flood of thoughts! What I imagined was going to be like a slow, waking-up process hit me like a mental flood. My mind clicked on, my mental mind

246

guy woke up, and in an attempt to make up for his absence, he flooded my thoughts with everything that had happened in the last twenty-four hours. I remembered everything and everyone. It was like being slapped back into consciousness. But the remembering was different, and I was filled with a strange lightness, a quiet energy that seemed to permeate somewhere deep inside of me.

I started to feel more alive, and I saw the world with amazing clarity. I felt like a part of me that had been asleep for my entire life had suddenly awakened and was looking out into the world for the first time, and that part of me was looking without labeling or judging. It was just seeing and appreciating and for the first time in my life I understood it all and I knew I was a part of everything and everything was a part of me. I smiled and was filled with so much emotion that tears rolled down my cheeks. I realized that the old me was gone forever, and then I saw a picture of Lisa in my mind, her dark, thick hair hanging beautifully around her full face. She was smiling as she was surrounded by a brilliant yellow light!

"My sunshine," I said under my breath. I turned to Andrea and asked, "Where is my phone?"

When we finally find our eternal light, when we discover who we really are, we will never walk in the land of darkness and unknowing ever again.

Printed in the United States
by Baker & Taylor Publisher Services